KNOCK ON MY DOOR

Books by **David Cullen**

The Eye of Makarios
The Mesrine Conclusion
The Windsor Secret
Pick Up Sticks
Knock On My Door
The Baalbeck Decision

KNOCK ON MY DOOR

DAVID CULLEN

Culpro Books

Knock On My Door
First published 2009

A version of this book was published as *Pick Up Sticks* in 2006

The author has asserted his right under the Copyright Designs and Patents Act 1988 to be identified as the author of this work.

ISBN: 978-0-9559911-3-4

www.lulu.com/davidcullen

Published Culpro Books
an imprint of Cullen Productions

The Song of Angel Baby

One and two	-	try on my shoe
Three and four	-	your key in the door
Five and six	-	use me for kicks
Seven and eight	-	masturbate
Nine and ten	-	I'll be home when?
Ten and one	-	the damage is done
Ten and two	-	what am I to you?
Ten and three	-	a graze on your knee
Ten and four	-	treat me as a whore
Ten and five	-	I am still alive
Ten and six	-	I'll pick up sticks
Ten and seven	-	I'll search for heaven
Ten and eight	-	feel my hate
Ten and nine	-	revenge is now mine

For the original 'Carly'
who knows who she is

10 years ago

"One, two, buckle my...?"

"Shoe!" The four year old boy – dead straight blonde hair falling down over his brow, blue eyes sparkling – smiled back at his mother. He clung tightly to the bag on his lap, careful that he did not drop it onto the dirty carriage floor as the rickety old train wobbled its way north from Grand Central Station. The bag contained a birthday present for his older sister, a horsey with a combable mane and an extendable tail. He had bought it (with a little help from Mommy's purse) in FAO Schwartz that afternoon. Now they had to get home quickly (before something called the 'rushower' Mommy said), hide the present and then go and pick up Sis from school. Mommy would help him wrap the present tomorrow.

"Three, four, knock on my...?"

"Door. How many more stops, Mommy?"

Mommy smiled. "How many did I say before?"

"Er... two."

"And how many times have we stopped since then?"

"Er... none?"

"That's right. So how many do we have left?"

He made a pout. "Three?" he grinned.

"Grr, you little..." Mommy leant across from the seat opposite and began tickling him under the arms.

The boy squirmed in his padded orange parka coat, and clung even tighter to the bag. In between squirms and giggles, he gasped "Mind the horsey, Mommy!"

Mommy stopped. She looked at her son with all the love in the world as she smoothed down his adorable blonde hair.

"One stop, that's all. One stop." She looked up around the empty train carriage. "Do you need the toilet before we get off?"

"No."

"I think I do. Look after the horse, I'll be back in a minute." Mommy picked up her purse and walked the six feet to the carriage toilet. She smiled back at her son as she closed the door.

That was the last time she ever saw him.

Introduction

"*Right. Ready?*"

"*As I'll ever be.*"

"*Now, we want you to tell us everything. A bit of background from your childhood and then from the time you first met him until this very moment. Tell us things just as they happened, don't embellish but leave nothing out, no matter how trivial it may seem. We want it all recorded. Can you do that?*"

"*Yes,*" *I nodded. This was what I had wanted for a long time, and yet suddenly I was afraid of my memories, afraid of the long-buried demons that might resurface.* "*Yes, I can.*"

"*Okay then.*" *Marinelli nodded towards the mirror.*

I took a deep breath.

So where do I begin? How much should I tell?

They say a lady should always have some secrets, layers which she allows to be peeled away only by the intimate few, a striptease that goes beyond the physical. The physical is the easy part. Taking your clothes off? No problem. The hard part is when the layers of your mind are stripped away also, level by level, until the very core of your being is exposed. And if that is attacked too, if the very essence of who you are is taken away, what are you left with? Nothing.

So how far shall I strip for you? How far should I go?

All the way?

I was born in Sausalito, California. My Dad worked in Silicon Valley, my Mom didn't do anything, except raise me and my older brother Clarke.

My parents divorced when I was two. Why, I don't know, they never did say – not in the children's hearing any way. And who cares about a catalyst? It's the end result that matters. I was just a little two year old girl, and all I knew was that Mom had gone from our lives. Dad was given custody of me and my brother. It would be twenty years before I saw my Mom again.

Even nowadays it is unusual to give sole custody to the father, so think of the surprise it caused then.

Dad had fought for us, got us – but what was he to do with us? He had a Very Important Job, he could not look after us alone. Mom was gone. A nanny was out of the question. So we were packed off to Dad's family: Clarke went to Granny's in Long Beach, California. I was sent to an aunt in Boston.

Aunty was married but she had no children. She was always unwell. In olden times she would have been one of those delicate women permanently draped on a chaisse-longue in her drawing room, kerchief always to hand, entertaining visitors – but only for a little while as the vapors would descend if she became tired or stressed.

Then suddenly Aunty had a child – me. No conception, no

gestation period, no early infancy – there I was, fully formed, descending upon her against my will. And against her will too.

What was childless Aunty to do with a little girl whom she had taken in only out of obligation to her brother?

The solution was obvious. The two words that strike fear into me even to this day: Boarding School.

I was sent to a small school out near Queensbury, New York, run by elderly women who believed in the use of firm – no, make that *extreme* – discipline. And I was to stay there for six years, from the age of four to the age of ten.

Sometimes I would 'go home for the holidays', but not always. Dad was always busy, often travelling the world for his company, and Aunty was often too ill to have me. So I spent a lot of holidays at school, even at Christmas.

I hated the place. The discipline would have put the Nazis to shame. And it seemed in inverse proportion to the 'crime'. Theft would be punished by a good talking to and the miscreant would be made to return their spoils (usually chocolate) to the owner. A minor transgression, like talking after lights out, was punished by 'solitary confinement' in a Wendy House for a month. And guess who was in there the most.

I came to loathe and love that Wendy House in equal measure. I loathed it because it was the instrument of punishment, the place where I was often forced to sleep, in the cold, without blankets, for weeks on end. I loved it because it was enclosed and secure – and I knew that once I was in there it would envelope me with its tightness, enclose me, protect me, womb-like, like the parents I didn't have.

There were other punishments. The slaps, the too-tight grip on the arm as I was hauled out of bed for daring to whisper to my friends, the scrubbings out.

And I could not complain. Who could I complain to? To my Dad, who had remarried when I was eight to a woman who behaved like the archetypal stepmother, who wanted to have my Dad to herself and have their own child? A woman who, when they did eventually have their own child, wanted me and my brother out of the family circle? Could I complain to my aunty, who was only interested in herself and whose level of sickness always increased the closer it got to school holidays?

And who would believe me anyway?

Oh, come on darling, we know you don't want to be at Boarding School, but there's no need to tell such stories. They can't possibly beat you like that. A month in a Wendy House at night? I ask you! Such an imagination! No, sorry, you can't come home at Christmas, Aunty is too ill and Daddy is travelling in Europe. I know it's upsetting, but it's best if you stay there. But the teachers are doing their best, there's no need to make up lies.

Make up lies... an allegation that has haunted me forever. Through my second Boarding School, from ten to eighteen. Through my time at nanny school at Grosse Point. Through my time training to be a make-up artist. Through my initial disastrous relationships with men. Through my depressions when my relationships ended.

And all I wanted was love. For someone to love me and to teach me how to give love back.

What was to happen in my life would make me long for my Boarding School days, when I knew when the beatings would come, when I knew what I did to 'deserve' to be punished. It would make me long for the security of the Wendy House, the cell for a little girl who only wanted someone, anyone, to love her.

Eventually my true friends believed me. Eventually the police and FBI believed me.

Will you believe me?

My name is Carly, and this is my story.

PART ONE

The One

1

It's funny how we get used to the norm, to the familiar – even when we know, deep down, that we dislike it. Nevertheless, we stick to it. Is it that we are too lazy to change – or too scared to?

I was with John for four and a half years. We shared an apartment in Queens, had a car, cats, a circle of friends – really quite the couple. But I wasn't happy. There was nothing wrong with John, in fact he was to turn out to be an even greater friend with what was to come. That happens with ex-lovers, doesn't it? You either split for a lifetime of mutual contempt, or you simply go your own ways and retain that mutual bond of people who have known total intimacy with each other.

But I always had the intuitive feeling that John was not The One. I did not know what the future held for me, but I knew it was not with John. And if The One was to come into my life, I could not be shacked up with Someone Else. I had to be free, to be ready for The One, ready for him to take me in his arms, ready for him to take me away, ready for him to make me complete.

Ready for love.

I had to be strong. And that meant ending my relationship with John. As it turned out, it was John who was the strong one. He probably saw the break-up coming – or perhaps he wanted out of it too. Whichever. We parted as amicably as possible. Not without snappy and bitchy remarks from both sides, but overall it did not descend into open warfare or even battle.

So there I was. Alone after four and a half years. For accommodation I moved in with a girlfriend, Barbara. But emotionally I was on my own. Situation Vacant – Only The One Need Apply.

I did wonder how long I was going to have to wait.

As it turned out, it was not long at all.

2

"God, what a shoot that was!" Clive ran his hands over his face in belated exasperation.

I looked at the overweight, grey-haired, middle-aged English photographer and nodded in agreement. "She's an absolute cow. True to her reputation." Cups in our hands, we went and sat at a wooden bench, looking out over the Hudson to Liberty Island beyond. The sun was hot, the sky relentlessly blue. Good for the photographer but not good for the make-up artist who kept having to touch up her clients (in the nicest possible way) every few minutes.

Clive sniffed ruefully. "Often Superbitches are really nice people, their reputations made up by the tabloids. But not this one. How did you manage to keep her looking so fresh?"

"Skill, my dear, skill. I ignore the rudeness and hysteria. I just say 'Yes' to whatever she demands, and then I do what I think is right. I'm the make-up artist, after all."

He sipped his coffee and then said, "You are brilliant at what you do, you know." A small, pencil-thin moustache of froth from his cappuccino decorated his upper lip.

"You've, er - " I moved my finger across my mouth.

"Oh, thanks." He licked his lip and then wiped it with the back of his hand. "I'll try and get you some more jobs. I think *Variety* will like what you've done with our Kate, maybe they'll use us as a team."

"But meantime I'd best not give up my day job." I smiled.

"You know what it's like, a crowded profession both for you and me."

"Yes, but you just happen to be one of the top photographers in the country."

"And you will be one of the top make-up artists. Believe me, Carly." After another swig of coffee, he asked "So how are things in Bloomingdale's?"

"Selling make-up is not as good as using it, but MAC pay well - "

"They need to, only employing fully-qualified make-up artists to sell their products."

"And it brings in a regular wage, unlike these freelance jobs."

There was a twinkle in Clive's eyes. "And what about your love life?"

"Clive!"

"What?" All innocence.

"My God, I've just broken up with John. I'm not ready for another relationship yet."

He reached forward and patted my hand. Could he tell I was lying? "Take the word of an old poof, darling – you are. I've known you for long enough, you're not the sort of person who can be alone for very long." There was something behind his smile.

"Oh no," I said, snatching back my hand. "Oh no, no, no. Don't tell me! You've got someone lined up for me."

He grinned. "What if I had?"

"Clive, I'm perfectly capable of conducting my own love life!"

"Really?"

No, not really, not at all. "Really."

"It's just some guy I know - "

"A guy you know?"

"Not in that way. I used to work with him in Australia. He's a very talented photographer. Might be your type. He's coming over to the States. I thought maybe you could show him around, until he gets his bearings."

"His *ball* bearings?"

"Dirty cow. But never turn your nose up at a good screw, angel."

"Clive," I said gently. "Thanks. I know you mean well. But I'm not interested."

"Okay, my love. I understand. But one day I'll get you paired off good and proper – before you get too old and your sales value decreases. Less commission for me!"

"You old goat. What's his name, anyway?"

"Who?"

"This friend of yours."

"Oh, the one you're not interested in?"

"Yep."

"Gary. Gary Goffrey."

3

"How are you, Clive?" I was standing in the lee of the doorway on the roof of Bloomingdale's on 59th Street. It was a chilly late October day and there were goose bumps on my arms – but this was the only place staff could come for a quick smoke, we were forbidden to stand in the street outside the shop.

"I've got a fucking sore arse, darling – but they won't let me stay in bed. That bitch of a staff nurse has had me up, walking about. When my cheeks move it feels like someone buggering me using a sandpaper condom."

"I'm not quite getting the picture here. Could you be more graphic?"

"Sorry, Heart, haemorrhoids have a habit of dulling one's descriptive powers."

I laughed as I looked across the rooftops of Manhattan. I just loved the English accent – and his way with words! I held my cellphone closer to my ear. "You in bed now?"

"No. They came and told me there was a call for me, but I had to go to the phone at the nurses' station, they wouldn't put it through to me. Said the walk would do me good. Now I'm standing here trying to keep my butt cheeks apart, hold the phone and talk to you at the same time. And all the nurses can do is giggle!"

I could hear people in the background. "Sadists."

"I tell you, some people I know would pay good money to be treated like this!"

"I won't keep you then. How long are you going to be in?"

"A couple of days. Usually you're out in one, but my Consultant wants to keep an eye on my rectum."

"Lucky boy."

"Who? Me or him?"

"Both of you. Can I come along and see you?"

"Darling, it would be wonderful."

"Tonight?"

"Perfect."

"I was thinking of bringing you some fruit – how about a large bunch of purple grapes? Your friends can nibble on them."

"Cow. That's how I ended up here in the first place."

The Bellevue Medical Center on 27th Street is thirty-two blocks from Bloomingdale's. The store doesn't close until 20:30 but I managed to beg some time off (my poor Uncle Clive was in a serious condition, didn't know whether he'd make it). By the time I had taken the Lexington IRT subway to 28th Street and then walked the one block south and four blocks east, it was past 21:00 when I arrived at the hospital.

Clive's room was up on the fourth floor. An imperious "Come!" answered my knock on the door. I went in.

Clive was sitting up in bed in his jim-jams, white cotton with red horny little devils all over them. Classy.

Two huge, unwrapped bouquets of flowers sat on a table, and his bedside cabinet was awash with cards. I was aware of someone sitting by the bed, probably one of his boyfriends, but my attention was on the invalid.

"Darling Carly!" Clive held out his arms.

"Hello, Clive," I gave him a huge hug and got the scrape of whiskery cheeks in return. "I decided against grapes," I explained as I pulled away. "Thought you could use these instead." I emptied six large bars of Ghirardelli dark chocolate onto the bed. Clive's favourite.

"Oh my God, you are sent from heaven, darling – appropriate for All Souls Day! You know I can't resist anything hard and black!" He grabbed a bar and began to rip off the brown wrapper.

"Nothing much wrong with him," I said to the other guy. "Not his mouth anyway."

The other guy smiled but did not say anything. He was rugged, rough dirty-handsome, a hillbilly-type character in an old black shirt and black jeans, thirty-ish, longish dark brown hair. And he had the most piercing green eyes I had ever seen. The sort of eyes that not only look at you but see right through you. Eyes that pierce your outer carapace and see into your very soul. Eyes that would probably shine in the dark.

Just for a moment I was taken aback. But then I realised this was just another example of the truth of the old adage: all the best looking men are gay.

"Hi," I said. "I'm Carly."

"Hi." That was all he said. One word, two letters, one syllable, a form of greeting, sounds like guy. Was he shy? Or just fucking rude?

I turned back to Clive, who was already halfway through the chocolate bar. "Like it then, do you, glutton?"

"Mm! Better than sex, darling. Stable, constant, you know what you're going to get and it goes into your mouth at the rate you dictate! And it tastes nicer."

"Thank you! Enough! I can see that you're better."

"Do you want to?" Clive was breaking up the remainder of the bar into separate pieces and putting them on the foil wrapper.

"What?"

"See it. My op."

"Er, no thanks, Clive. A tempting offer, and really kind of

you, but I'll leave that to others." Before I could stop myself, I had looked across at Rough Handsome and back again. It was a glance of only one nano-second, but Clive caught it. He smiled mischievously.

"Fancy some?" His eyebrows raised, Mr Innocent. Then he held out the foil. "Chocolate, I mean."

"Thanks." I took a piece.

Clive offered the foil to Rough Handsome, but he shook his head.

"I need a pee. Hold this for me, will you darling?" Clive thrust the foil towards me as he pulled back the sheets.

I took the foil and stood up to let him swing his legs out. "You okay?" I asked. "Need any help?" Rough Handsome did not move to assist his friend.

"No, thank you, darling. They've had me up and down all day. I'm okay as long as I'm careful."

I didn't know what to expect. Maybe I thought they would have him in a dressing, bandaged up so that it looked like he was wearing a diaper. But it was just the normal Clive who slowly, gingerly made his way across to the ensuite bathroom. I think he had lost a pound or two, and I noticed a couple of maroon splotches on the back of his jammie trousers, which were blood stains not horny little devils. He made it to the bathroom and closed the door behind him.

I turned back and again gave a little inward start as I saw the impossibly green eyes looking at me.

"Hell of a guy, Clive," I blurted. Why was I feeling nervous?

"A nice bloke." Rough Handsome actually spoke, and he smiled – a wide, charming, come-to-bed smile. I felt my pantie elastic tremble. He had some sort of an accent, but his voice was so soft I couldn't make out what it was.

"Known him long?" I asked.

"Only professionally."

"Oh, you're not - " *Shit, what was I saying?* "You – you're in the business?"

"I'm a photographer. I've just come over to the States. Clive's found me a place to rest. I don't really know anyone here, apart from him."

"Oh. Right. Where are you from? I can hear an accent but I can't place it."

"Australia. If I was to say," his voice changed, louder and coarse, "'Put another kangaroo on the barbie, Sheila', would that help?"

I laughed. No, it didn't help. What the hell had he just said? But I was gracious. "Well, welcome to America."

"Thanks. And what about you?" The eyes were now smiling at me, they had decided I was friend not foe. "What do you do?"

"I'm a make-up artist. I freelance and I also work for MAC at Bloomingdale's. Heard of them?"

"MAC, no. Bloomingdale's? Is that a shop? I'm just an ignorant Aussie."

"You're a rather desirable Aussie," I wanted to say, but my mouth was stopped from embarrassing me by a shout from the bathroom.

"Christ!" It was followed by a fart of such proportions that the earth's crust must have moved. "Fucking hell!" shouted Clive.

I dashed over to the bathroom door. "Clive, you okay?" Nothing. "Clive?"

"I'm okay, love," came the voice from within. He was actually out of breath. "That's better out than in, as the actress said to the butt plug."

The door opened and I stepped back quickly.

"My arse will be the death of me," announced Clive as he walked with a slightly bandy gait back across the room. Carefully, he sat back down on the edge of the bed. He winced as he swung his legs back between the sheets.

I covered him over.

"Thanks, Angel." He reached for his chocolate. "I haven't

introduced you two, have I? Gary, this is Carly. Carly, this is my friend Gary Goffrey."

"Hi Carly," said Rough Handsome. "That's Godfrey without a D."

"And this," said Clive, "is Carly without a boyfriend."

Try on my shoe

He sat hugging his knees in the corner of the locked studio apartment. It was dark outside and the only light came from his small pocket torch sitting on the floor beside him and pointing up into his face. His breathing was deep and nervous, occasionally catching on the inhale. Almost a sob.

Georgie was a shy, jumpy, introverted child, his face plain and unemotional. Any spark of character had long ago been beaten out of him by the man he knew as Daddy. He had known no one else. Ever. No brothers, no sisters, no friends – not even a mother. Just Daddy. Daddy was not here right now, but Georgie could still hear his voice, forever in his head.

You want to go out and play with the children, boy? No way, kiddo. Too dangerous. You remember that time we did let you out? Remember what you did? Christ, they nearly caught you that time. If I hadn't come back, the authorities would have had you and they would have taken you away and locked you up. Even so, we still had to flee the area, didn't we? And all because of you, you little creep.

And then Daddy would start to hurt him. Bang, bang, banging his head against the wall. Sometimes there were just two bangs. Other times, when Daddy's rages were fierce, the bangs would go on and on and on. There was even that one time, where they used to live, when he banged his head against the mirror and the glass broke, cutting his forehead and making him bleed. But still Daddy didn't stop banging. Not until he was sated.

Georgie rested his chin on his knees, held his legs tightly and began to rock backwards and forwards.

The harsh, sharp light from the torch cast black shadows over his face. He smiled to himself. Daddy could hurt him all he wanted, but Daddy didn't know his little secret. His precious little secret.

Daddy didn't know that sometimes he managed to get out of this room, even though he was locked in.

And Daddy didn't know about the clothes. The big boy's clothes, the man's clothes, that he sometimes put on when Daddy wasn't around.

Right now he had his short pants on, but he was wearing a pair of Daddy's shoes. Big man's shoes. He moved his feet - the shoes felt so big! Would he ever fit them? Would he ever be able to fill Daddy's shoes?

Suddenly he stopped rocking and the smile fell from his face. He had that feeling again. He grabbed the torch and shone it across the room onto the locked door.

It was Daddy. He was coming back. Georgie hoped he would be in a good mood tonight. Daddy had been out most of the day. Wonder if he had brought him anything to play with? Or anyone?

He turned off the torch and let the darkness of the room envelope him. Wrapping his hands back around his legs, he began the slow rocking again. Gently and with his pure voice of a child, he began to sing softly.

"One, two, buckle my shoe..."

4

After I left the hospital that night I didn't give Rough Handsome Gary a second thought.

I'm lying, of course.

I must have caught a cab. I must have paid the driver when I got out. I must have exchanged words with the doorman. I must have had a nightcap with Barbara, my friend who was putting me up. But I wasn't aware of it.

All I was aware of was the soft, calming voice and those piercing green eyes staring at me, smiling at me. Undressing me?

Wow, Mr Godfrey without a D, you certainly know how to make an impression on a girl – and so effortlessly. You were pleasant, charming, but you couldn't have been more indifferent towards me if you tried.

Still, you were something for a girl with a twitchy right hand to think about as she lay in her bed. Dream candy.

But we had not exchanged phone numbers or e-mail addresses. I'd said goodbye after half an hour. Clive was coming out of hospital the next day and I wouldn't be seeing him unless and until we had another job together or our paths crossed at an agency promotion or something.

So Mr Godfrey without a D was a fleeting pleasantness. A momentary diversion. Nothing more. He was gone from my life.

Or so I thought.

It was just four days later. I was in work, behind the MAC counter on the main floor of Bloomingdale's, on the bway. There were three MAC Girls and one MAC Boy working that morning, each of us easily identifiable in the MAC uniform of black. Black what didn't matter – as long as it was black. So although we were all 'uniform' we were each dressed differently. I was in a black button-up blouse and short straight skirt.

It was Thursday, and I was working the full shift from 10:00 to 20:30. Which meant long day.

I was crouching down behind the counter, struggling with a new box of NW25 Foundation bottles which were refusing to leave the drawer, when I was aware of a shadow above.

"Jac," I called over my shoulder. "Customer."

Beautiful, blonde, frizzy Jacqui, my colleague and friend, seemed hesitant. "I think the customer wants you, Carly," she said.

"Oh?" I looked up from my crouching position and then gasped as I fell back onto my butt, the foundation bottles rolling out over the floor. My unladylike position reassured the customer that the MAC uniform stretched to black panties as well.

I forgot about trying to close my legs as I looked up into two piercing green eyes. "Oh!"

Rough Handsome Gary smiled down at me but said nothing.

I leapt to my feet, brushing my skirt down, straightening the collar of my blouse, unconscious nervous grooming. "Gary, it's you. Hi." Did I sound too girlish?

"Carly, it is you."

"Yes, it is me," I said fatuously. *Listen to yourself!*

"So this is where you work, I didn't know."

You didn't? I thought I'd told you.

"I was just passing," he continued. "Having an explore of the area. I saw the MAC products in the window..."

"And here you are." I was aware of Jacqui trying not to look at me, a wicked grin splitting her face.

"Here I am," he agreed. "You free for a drink?"

Wow! Prevaricate why don't you?

"Er..."

"What time do you go for lunch?"

"One."

"Okay, I'll see you then." And with that he turned and walked away, not waiting for a response. Typical, confident, arrogant male. I watched him go. In his black jeans and black leather jacket he could have been auditioning for a job with MAC.

But I had the feeling that I was the one being auditioned.

I was still admiring his departing hips when I felt a presence next to me.

"And that was?" smiled Jacqui.

I was momentarily away with my thoughts. "That was..." I looked at Jac. "That, I think, was opportunity knocking. Potential?"

"Potential," agreed my friend.

"Sex or shoulder?" I wondered.

"Sex definitely. Shoulder? Don't know," mused Jacqui. "He didn't have much to say, which is a good sign. You'll have to find out, won't you? At lunchtime."

And find out I did. Gary reappeared at exactly one o'clock and we went upstairs to the Showtime Cafe on Floor 7½. Over exceptionally large glasses of Beaujolais, we talked.

With hindsight, I seem naïve. But at the time I was amazed and overwhelmed. Amazed that after four years with John, no sooner was I free than I was attracting male attention again. Me! Amazed that Gary had sought me out, despite his story of just exploring the area. Amazed that I had freed myself to wait for

The One and straightaway fate had sent this man knocking on my counter top.

And overwhelmed by those amazing green eyes. Eyes that seemed already to know more about me than I did, eyes that demanded to be told every detail of my life. All Gary asked was "Are you in a relationship, Carly?", and that opened the verbal floodgates. I told him everything, all about my early life, all about my previous love affairs, about splitting up with John. Poor Gary, he must have been bored. But he didn't show it. Those eyes maintained their interest, their hold, throughout.

And then suddenly it was two o'clock. Lunch break over. Had I actually stopped talking at all during the last hour? I didn't think so, but my glass was empty and there were the remnants of something on a plate on the table, so I must have shut up at some stage if only momentarily.

Gary walked me back down to the MAC counter.

"Meet me," he said.

"Yes," I said without hesitation. "I would like that."

"Tuesday night. What time do you finish?"

"Eight-thirty."

"I'll meet you outside."

"Okay."

He turned and left. No touch, no handshake, no kiss. And yet as I stood there and watched his hair get caught by the wind as he opened the main door and walked out into Lexington Avenue, I felt a warm, all over glow. It was as if we had just spent an hour of passion, as if I had been a willing partner in my own seduction and was now enjoying the after affects. Must have been the Beaujolais.

I turned back to the counter, and there was Jacqui with the dirtiest, most salacious grin I had ever seen. She was expecting me to say something but I just smiled.

"Well?" she asked.

The box of foundation bottles was underneath the counter where I had left it. I began taking the bottles out and lining them up on the display behind. "Mm...?"

"Sex or shoulder?" said Jacqui. "Tell me."

I tried to keep the game going but I couldn't. I smiled. "Shoulder? Most definitely. For a man he's one hell of a good listener. Very unusual. Sex? Jac, I have a feeling we will find that out very soon..."

5

It took two days for the euphoria of my lunch with Gary to wear off. During that time I had those thoughts that all of us girls have about new male acquaintances. If you are a girl, you know what those thoughts are. If you are a man, that's a secret of the sisterhood that you are never to be told.

I was happier than I had been in a long time. Two days since I had seen Gary, three days until I saw him again.

Only when I was going over things for the umpteenth time in my head, reliving the Thursday lunch, considering the possibilities, the various scenarios, that might happen on Tuesday night, did I realise something.

He had asked me questions and I had replied willingly, eagerly. No fact too personal, no remembrance too intimate. Gary knew everything about me.

About Gary I knew nothing whatsoever.

6

Tuesday. I honestly thought it would never come. Why does time do that? When you are enjoying yourself, time flies. When you are *waiting* to enjoy yourself, time drags.

Time is a perverse bastard.

But Tuesday came at last. I was excited, and I had that first date nervousness.

I wanted to be outside Bloomie's waiting for him (no shy turning up acceptably late for this emancipated lady), but some last minute bitch – sorry, *customer* – who took forever to agree with me that *Mulch* eyeshadow did not suit her, delayed me.

So it was 20:40 before I left.

And Gary was not there waiting for me.

Shit.

I stood outside the main doors in the dark of that November evening, the buses on Lexington crawling past, brightly lit from within, the glum looking-but-not-seeing faces of the passengers inside each in their own worlds with their own problems. But I bet none of them had been stood up by a Rough Handsome Aussie Stud tonight.

Further up the Avenue, on the corner with 59th Street, stood another lone figure. He looked like a gay, waiting for his boyfriend. Well, I thought, I hope you have more luck tonight than I've had, pal. He had short, close-cut hair, and wore a black stripy shirt and jeans so tight and savagely pulled up in the crotch that they must have been strangling him. And he had on the same sort of black leather jacket that Gary had been wearing the other day.

I looked away as our eyes met. And then I frowned. Not only was he wearing the same leather jacket as Gary had, but he had the same piercing green eyes as well.

As I looked back he was coming towards me, smiling.

"Hi Carly."

"Gary?"

"Well I was the last time I looked."

Well you weren't the last time I looked. "You, er… You've had your hair cut."

"I thought I'd smarten up. I haven't been out with a real lady for a long, long time."

Immediately I felt like a cow. A prize heffer. There I was, mentally dissing him, even thinking he was gay. And all the poor guy had done was tidy himself up to look good for his date. So what if his dress-sense left a lot to be desired – he was Australian for God's sake!

Thank God he couldn't read my mind.

"You look nice," I lied with the best of intentions.

"Thanks. So do you. Good enough… to eat. Shall we?"

"What?"

"Eat."

"Oh! Oh, yes. Anywhere you particularly fancy?" Don't be an idiot, Carly, he was new to the country.

"I saw a little Italian place round on 59th. You like Italian?"

"Love it. Let's eat then."

He crooked his arm and I accepted the invitation to link him.

"And this time," I said. "I want to know everything about *you*."

So why did I end up talking about myself all over again?

Over a delicious *tagliatelli al forno* in Bottega del Vino Restaurant, we talked. Gary did get a word in edgeways this time (or was it that this time I managed to get him to say something?). He was a photographer, I knew that already. He was also a writer, writing about photography and photographers, that sort of thing. He had helped set up a photography magazine in Australia. It was good work and good money, and he was hoping to do the same thing here in the States.

And it was with our mutual friend Clive that Gary hoped, as he put it, to do business. Meantime he was writing freelance articles and hawking them around the already-established magazines. He was also practising web site design.

But always the conversation seemed to turn back to me. He had a way of making me feel important, like I was the only person in the world that mattered. Those piercing green eyes transfixed me and I felt like I was the centre of his universe. He made me feel calm, relaxed. I knew I could confide in him, like he was my oldest friend.

"You know, Gary," I said as I drained the last mouthful of our second bottle of *Barolo* and picked up the rather blurred cup of espresso in front of me. "You have a way of making me feel special."

"That's because you *are* special, Carly. Very special. In fact, you are one of the most special people I have ever met."

And with that Rough Handsome Gary Goffrey without a D reached over and took both my hands in his. The piercing green eyes looked into mine. "Come back to my place," he said.

"Sure," I said.

Sex or shoulder?

Both. Definitely.

Your key in the door

Georgie sat hugging his knees in the corner of the studio. It was two in the morning and the place was so, so dark. But really that was the way he liked it. He had his torch for when he needed to see something, but long ago he had learnt not to be afraid. The darkness was his friend. He was always kept in the dark.

He breathed oh so quietly. No catching sobs this time because he knew Daddy was nearby.

Daddy had returned four hours ago, and he had not been alone. He had brought someone home with him. Georgie had heard them talking, laughing, as they came up the stairs. And as the key turned in the door, he had hidden himself away quickly. Daddy had always told him he must never be seen. *Little children must be not seen and not heard.* Or else.

But he had watched. Watched as they drank wine together (horrible, sour stuff), watched as they had kissed, watched as Daddy had taken his friend's clothes off, watched as Daddy had taken his own clothes off, watched as – mercy, what was the friend doing to Daddy? It looked like she was eating him!

That must hurt! Daddy!

But no. Daddy had his eyes closed and was smiling and

making groaning noises. He seemed to be enjoying himself. He was being eaten and he was enjoying it!

Then the friend stopped, and she laid back on the bed.

And that was when Daddy got his revenge.

And Georgie liked that.

Daddy poked himself into his friend. And she gasped and said "Oh God." But Daddy did not stop. He got faster and faster, poking himself harder and rougher into his friend. Making her groan, making her shout. Making her scream.

Go, Daddy, go! Teach her a lesson she'll never forget.

Hurt the bitch, Daddy.

7

Is there such a thing as instant love? At that time, I thought there was.

After our first date, our first passionate but tentative do-you-like-this? lovemaking, we saw each other with the increasing regularity of the infatuated. First there was a four day gap, then a three day gap, then a two day gap. Quite simply, we could not get enough of each other.

Most times, nature permitting (and on one occasion when it didn't), we ended up back at Gary's rented, run-down studio in TriBeCa, for two or three hours of lovemaking.

The sex was good, Gary was good, but I did not stay a complete night at the place. There was something about the room that gave me the creeps. Gary had lived there only for a few weeks, so he had not yet had time to put his personality into the place; it was impersonal and unhomely. It was as if the studio itself was a third entity, and I felt it was watching us, listening to us, and disapproving.

Tough.

The studio had a bed, and that was all I needed right now. Me, a bed… and the man with the piercing green eyes with whom I had fallen madly in love.

8

No matter when I arranged to meet Gary, no matter what time, no matter how early I turned up, he was always there waiting for me. Since the shock of his appearance on our first date, I had become used to him wearing all black. Same jeans, same shoes, same leather jacket, a variety of different shirts – but always all black.

The day I arranged to meet him at Grand Central Terminal was to be one I would remember forever.

I entered the station from Vanderbilt Avenue and stood for a moment on the West Balcony. This place always amazed me. Often I would rush through it, head down, like most New Yorkers, but on those rare times like today when I just stood and looked at it, I was almost overwhelmed by its cavernous beauty. I could see Gary waiting by the ornate, clock-topped Information island in the centre of the concourse. His back was towards me, but I waved anyway.

My heart thumped. I was in love.

I skipped down the stairs and manoeuvred my way through the midday crowds.

I tapped him on the shoulder. "Hi, Gary."

He turned, and those amazing eyes looked straight into my soul. "Hi, Angel Baby," he smiled. And then he said, "Will you marry me?"

∞

I don't think I actually passed out. I certainly did a tiny bit of pee in my pants, I can recall that clearly.

I remember Gary leading me to The Grand Central Oyster Bar on the lower level. I remember more than one bottle of red wine on the table. I remember – for some reason, quite distinctly – a plate full of Cajun grilled catfish filet with steamed red bliss potatoes in front of me. I remember the food slowly disappearing – it must have gone into my mouth, but I have no recollection of eating.

There was a haze around me and my world. The impenetrable mist of love. I could see no further than the man sitting opposite me. The man who had come into my life and with four words had expunged the memories of my unhappiness: the divorce of my parents, the Boarding Schools, the failed relationships, the depressions.

Rough Handsome Mr Gary Goffrey without a D.

My future husband.

We went back to his creepy studio where the walls had eyes. But I didn't care. I was with my husband. He would look after me.

Gary had some more red wine waiting for us, and we drank and made love.

And this time I did stay the night.

When I awoke the next morning, Gary was already up. I could hear voices, like two people, in the separate kitchen area. One low voice, one high voice, could have been a girl or a child. The conversation was animated.

Slowly I sat upright on the side of the bed. I stood up and gasped as cramps shot through my stomach. Shit, exactly how much had I had last night? Drink, I mean. I knew exactly how much sex I had had, Gary's flaky residue was stuck to various parts of my body.

The pain subsided as I stood up straight. I waited to take a couple of breaths and then I walked across to the door of the kitchenette. I was about to turn the handle when I realised I was naked. If we had a visitor I didn't want to shock them first thing in the morning! And anyway, from now on my body was for my husband's eyes only.

There were no towels or bathrobes about, so I found my jeans and top across the other side of the room (where they had been flung the night before) and, suitably covered, I went into the kitchen.

Gary was in there on his own, plunging the plunger on a cafetière. He smiled as he looked at me. "Hi, Angel Baby."

"Good morning," I went across and kissed him. "I thought there was somebody else here."

"No, just me."

"I heard voices. I thought you were talking to someone."

"Oh, my silly Angel Baby. That was the radio!" He nodded to a small transistor on the shelf above the sink. "Scion Radio. I usually put it on for company. I forgot I wasn't on my own anymore."

I encircled his waist with my arms as he poured out the coffee. I could smell him through his clean black shirt.

"You won't be on your own ever again," I said. "My husband."

9

"Carly, are you sure you want to do this?" My Dad was talking from France, where he now lived, but the connection was so good he could have been in the next room.

"Dad, I love him. He's the one I've been waiting for."

"But you don't know anything about him!"

"I know enough. I know who he is, what he does."

"But marriage is a big step. Can't you just live together?"

"We will be. He's moving in with me at Barbara's while we look for a place of our own."

There was a pause, then Dad said "I'm only concerned for you, darling. I don't want you to make a mess like I did."

"That wasn't your fault."

"It was everyone's fault. Just please think carefully. Marriage is not something to be rushed into. Any idea of a date yet?"

"Three weeks time. December 22nd."

"Carly, are you sure you want to do this?"

Not another one! This time it was Clive. He had called me at work – a strict no-no – but Jacqui had taken over my customer and I was pretending I was taking a mail order call.

I spoke lowly. "Clive! You were the one who introduced us in the first place."

"Yes, because I thought pussy was lonely, Sweetheart. I

didn't intend for you to marry him."

"And you're going into business with him."

"That's not the same as marriage, dear. I'll make sure *I'm* not shafted."

"Why is it," I tried to keep the anger from my voice, "that people keep telling me to be careful? Why can't everyone be happy for me? I'm getting married, for God's sake."

"Are you sure he's not just marrying you for your passport or residency? It would help with his business plans."

"He loves me. He says he's never met anyone like me."

"What do you know about him?"

"Enough."

"Do you know about the drugs in Australia?"

For a moment I said nothing. Should I put the phone down now? "What drugs?" I asked slowly.

"He used to hang around with people who were doing drugs and things in Australia. And I'm not talking about recreational users."

"Clive, you're being stupid," I didn't care if he heard my sharpness. "Gary is so straight, there's no way he would be involved in anything like that. I am living with him, remember? If he was a junkie, I would know. He doesn't do drugs."

"Okay, Carly Heart, okay. I just wanted to put up a little warning flag for you."

"I've got to go."

"Just be careful, darling."

"Jac, am I doing the right thing?"

We were having lunch in the Showtime Café up on Floor 7½, sitting at the same table as Gary and I had sat at. No wine this time, just a Diet Coke and a panini for each of us.

"You having doubts?" asked my bubbly friend.

"Me? No, not at all. I love the guy. But there've been a few people now who have questioned what I'm doing."

Jacqui took a sip of her drink. "Well, it has been very quick.

You were four and a half years with John, and now within four and a half weeks of being with Gary you're going to marry him."

"Your point is...?"

"My point is..." Jacqui was obviously choosing her words carefully. She thought, then she smiled and reached across and touched my hand. "My point is, you're my best friend. You've always been there for me. And I trust your judgement. You really love this guy - "

"Oh, yes."

"Then go for it. You've always said that John wasn't The One, that you'd know him when he came along. So if he's come along, why wait?"

My body relaxed as I sighed. "Thanks, Jac. That's what I want to hear. People just don't understand, do they?"

"They're only thinking of you. We do love you, you know."

"I know." I popped the last piece of my panini into my mouth.

Then Jacqui said, "Just one thing."

"What?"

"Be careful, Carly. Be careful, and be very, very sure."

10

Did I have any doubts? Absolutely not. But what Clive had said bounced around in my head like a pinball.

We had ordered To Go from Sbarro and we were back in Gary's studio. He had poured us a glass each of the ubiquitous red wine, which helped the lasagne and cheesecake go down a treat.

I broached the subject as I tidied up the detritus from the small coffee table, cramming everything back into the Sbarro sack it came in. "Gary, honey, can I ask you something?"

"Of course, Angel Baby, anything."

"You might not like it, but I need to ask."

His expression remained calm, open, loving. "What is it?"

"Something Clive said. That you used to hang around with a lot of druggies in Australia."

All expression fell from his face. His bottom lip quivered. "Oh God, no." He put his head in his hands. "Oh, God." I thought my fiancé was going to cry.

"Gary?" I reached across. His hands were cold.

He took hold of my fingers as he brought his hands back down onto his lap. The green eyes looked straight at me. "Carly, I'm sorry. I'm so, so sorry. I didn't want to have to tell you – No, no, let me speak. It was the reason I left Australia. My business went down the drain. Some people where I was living, who I thought were my friends, they stole all my stuff, my camera, equipment, computers, everything. Sold them for drugs." He was quiet. Should I say anything? Then he continued, "Looking back now, I feel like a fool. I was too gullible. That's why I'm now more cautious when I meet people. What little stuff I had left I put into storage, and I decided to get the hell out of the country. To make a clean start. On the other side of the world. I feel so silly to let myself be used like that, that's why I didn't tell you."

We were still holding hands. My Gary, my baby boy, seemed so sad. I tried to look into his heart, but I could not get beyond those green, green eyes. I hoped I sounded reassuring. "I knew it must have been something like that. I knew you wouldn't be involved with such people. I know you, don't I?" I smiled. "You're my husband, my baby. But you should have told me, I don't want to be finding out things from other people."

"I'm sorry, Angel Baby."

"Just promise me there's no more secrets. Or if there is, please tell me now."

He looked into my eyes. "Perhaps I should tell you everything…"

11

At last I found out about him. Whether he would ever have told me had I not pressed, I don't know. Why are men always so damn secretive?

Gary Goffrey had been born in Melbourne, Australia, thirty-two years previously. He was the middle child of three boys.

Like most young men, he had done a variety of jobs in his late teens including – don't laugh, and yes seriously – sheep shearing. But photography had always been his passion: light, form, composition. Landscape and still life were all well and good, but he had come to specialise in the human body. He regarded it as the ultimate creation, a temple to God. He had become quite well known and respected as a fashion photographer in New South Wales.

Then he had fallen for one of his models. Her name – again don't laugh – was Sheila. He had thought it was the match of the century. They had moved in together, and he thought they would be getting married. Then one day she had upped and left him. She said that she didn't love him anymore, that she had 'moved on'. The moving she was actually doing was upwards - with her career. She had used Gary, and he had taken her far. But for Sheila it was not far enough. A day after leaving Gary, she had gotten herself an high-profile agent – and she had moved in with him by the weekend.

Sheila's leaving hurt Gary hard, and it contributed in no small way to the downward spiral in his business. He just didn't have the inspiration any more – his muse had left him.

This on top of the thefts by the druggies led to him having a minor breakdown – and his departure from Australia.

"There," he said. "That's everything." His eyes were red rimmed, and they looked so plaintive.

I couldn't think of anything to say. So I just leant forward and kissed him.

12

It was natural that we would move in with each other before the wedding. Although I had now stayed several nights in Gary's studio, I was not prepared to move in there permanently – the place gave me the creeps with its watching walls. They say walls have ears; these had eyes as well.

So Gary moved in with me at Barbara's on the Upper West Side. Babs didn't mind (I think she was pleased with the extra rent), and we were discreet, keeping our more open displays of lust until we were alone in our room.

Gary kept on his studio, considerate enough not to move his things so that we didn't clutter up Barbara's apartment. He went back there daily. He had bought some computer equipment and a camera from money I had loaned him, and he was slowly working on the foundations of his new business: a publishing and library web site for photographers.

It was just before lunchtime on the Thursday two weeks before our wedding that my stomach cramps started again.

The shops of Manhattan were busy with the pre-Christmas rush, and Bloomie's was throbbing with customers. I hadn't sat down all morning. Maybe it was that that started it. Or maybe it was the sushi of the night before. Or the one-more-glass-than-I-should-have of red wine. I wasn't due my period, so it wasn't that.

Whatever. The pain was so severe that it made me gasp out loud as I was serving a customer (*Atlas satin* eye shadow).

Jacqui heard me and dashed over. "Carly?"

"I'm sorry," I apologised to the customer. "Jac, can you help this lady? Women's things." I smiled weakly as my fellow members of the sisterhood nodded in understanding.

The staff toilet seemed further away than usual, but I finally found the sanctuary of a cubicle.

A fart shot out as I pulled down my pants. Was that all it was? (I had always been notorious amongst my friends for the tornado-like abilities of my rectum.) For a moment I felt marginally better, but then the gripping pain returned with avengeance.

I peed. No relief, but Madame Pussy felt strangely sticky as I stood up. Half bending over, I looked down.

The toilet was covered in blood.

13

Jacqui was an angel. I wanted to wait until our Manager returned from lunch, but Jac wouldn't have any of it. I was coated, scarved, gloved and packed off home right away, with strict instructions not to come in tomorrow if I wasn't better.

The apartment was empty. Barbara was out at work and Gary was down at his studio.

A nice cup of Earl Grey tea (they know a thing or two, these Brits), a couple of tylenol and a lie down was all I needed, I told myself.

I must have dozed off for a few minutes, but then I was awoken by screaming. Loud and screeching. *What the hell?*

I sat up, looking around the room. Was someone else in the apartment with me? Where was it coming from?

It took ten long seconds before I realised that the screaming was coming from me. My stomach was on fire. It felt like I had been skewered and was being spit-roasted.

I needed the hospital, and fast.

My cellphone was broken (Gary kept promising me he'd buy me a new one), so I hastily scribbled a note on a scrap of paper:

Gary / Babs,
Pain in stomach. Gone to St Vincent's. Whoever
gets home first, please come down there - I don't
want to be alone.
Carly xx

St Vincent's Hospital down on West 12th Street was the nearest emergency facility, not the New York-Presbyterian up on 220th and Broadway. It took me an hour to get down there, I could have died in that time (and people have). I tried very hard not to let the cab driver see how bad I was, in case he threw me out midtown. As it was he was indifferent (like most New York cab drivers) – and he didn't speak English (like...).

Waiting. Checking-in. Triaged. Called. Prods, probes, open wide for an internal (smile and say "Cheese!") to ensure I was not pregnant, ectopic or otherwise, and a urine infection was diagnosed.

They gave me two huge tablets, so big they would have had difficulty giving them to a bull as a pessary, and a bottle of smaller cousins to take three times a day – and remember to complete the course. And lay off the alcohol while you were taking them, and maybe sex as well.

The tablets kicked in like a mule, and after fifteen minutes rest and a further fifteen minutes paperwork I was allowed to go home.

I must say that I felt so much better, if a little shell-shocked, as I left the hospital and searched for a cab.

I must also say that in the four hours I was at the hospital, neither Babs nor Gary had come to be with me.

14

I got home at 22:45.

Babs was out. Gary was in the bedroom. I was in a state of fury.

Gary looked up from his magazine. "Hi, Angel Baby, you're late." The smile dropped from his face as he saw the Queen of the Valkyries standing in the bedroom doorway. "Carly?"

"And where the fuck were you?"

He looked perplexed. "What? I've been at the studio, you know that."

"Why didn't you come to the hospital?"

"What hospital? What are you talking about?"

"I've just been at St Vincent's for four fucking hours. Didn't you read my note?"

"What note?" He shook his head. "I'm sorry, I don't understand. I thought you were working late at the shop." He swung his legs over the edge of the bed.

"I left you a note! Telling you I was ill and was going to hospital and asking you to come down."

"Angel Baby, I didn't see any note."

"I left it on the coffee table in the living room!"

"Oh my God, my poor little baby, are you okay?" He stood up and came over to me, arms open. But I wasn't having any of it.

"I left you a note," I said more lowly as I turned away from his arms and back into the living room. "On the coffee table, over there..."

Deflation. There was nothing on the glass coffee table. Not even an old magazine or a used cup. "Did you move it?"

"I haven't moved anything, Angel Baby. I didn't see any note."

"But I left it there."

He came up behind me and hugged me. "As long as you're all right, that's the important thing." He nuzzled into my neck. "My precious baby."

"I left a note. I know I did," I started to cry, small sobs of frustration. "Gary, I was so alone."

"Darling, I'm here," he turned me around and lifted up my chin. "You will never be alone again."

And, as always, those green eyes just melted me.

Barbara came home an hour later. Gary was back in the bedroom, reading his magazines ("Research," he said. "To see what my rivals are doing."). In the meantime I had searched the living room from top to bottom. There was no note to be found anywhere. It had not fallen on the floor, it had not blown under any chair, it had not grown legs and leapt on top of the book shelves. It was like it had never existed. *Like I was imagining that I wrote it.*

Barbara could see that I looked both pale and red-eyed, and she expressed her concern. "Carly, you okay?"

I told her about the stomach pains and about the trip to the hospital. "Babs," I tried to sound conversational, keep it light. "Is this your first time home tonight? Or did you come in and go back out again?"

She frowned. "I came in at five, went back out at six. I've been round Karen's. Why?"

"Was Gary in when you came home?"

She nodded. "Yes, he was in your room."

"You didn't see a note I left on the table, did you?"

"A note?"

"Asking one of you to come down to the hospital to be with me?"

She shook her head. "There wasn't any note when I came home."

I sighed. "This is so strange… Well, never mind. It's all over now. I'll live!"

"Have you eaten?"

"No, after the pain I didn't feel like anything. I could murder a coffee, though."

"I'll make it for you."

"And," I called as she went into the kitchen, "a chocolate cookie?"

I sat there with my thoughts. I *had* written that note. Hadn't I? I thought I had, but maybe I was so blinded by pain I didn't know what I was doing.

I looked at the bedroom door, behind which was my future husband. I looked over towards the kitchen where my dear friend was making my coffee. I looked down at my own lap.

Gary, Barbara, Carly.

One of us was lying.

Use me for kicks

Georgie sat hugging his knees in the corner of the studio. It was daytime but you wouldn't know it. The curtains were pulled tight closed and the room was coated in dark grey shadow.

He rocked back and forth, his chin resting on the rough skin of his knees. He wasn't happy.

Daddy had said they had come to this new land to get away from things. To get away from the trouble Daddy said he had caused, 'Down Under'. Daddy had said it would be just the two of them - but now this bitch had come along to spoil things.

Daddy would come home during the day, but he was hardly ever here at night any more. He never came to look after Georgie when it was dark and the monsters came out. Was Daddy just using him? Didn't Daddy love him any more?

Yesterday Daddy had had a screaming fit, punching and kicking him, telling him that he would never come out of this room, never, ever. Not any more. This was a new life for Daddy, and Daddy wanted to make a go of it.

But then Daddy had calmed down. He had even laughed. He had some sort of paper in his hand, a note, and he kept looking at it, giggling.

And then had come the shocker.

Daddy had told Georgie that he was going to have a new Mommy. Wasn't that good? The three of them would live happily ever after. But Georgie would still need to keep quiet – his new Mommy didn't know about him yet. He would still need to be locked away – until the time was right.

Now Georgie stopped rocking. He nodded. Yes, they would be moving. Yes, he would move from this room to his new one.

He smiled.

And yes Daddy, the monsters will be coming with me.

15

As the wedding got closer I expected to get more and more nervous, for the doubts to increase. But they did not. In fact, the opposite happened. As I spent more and more time, more and more nights, with my Rough Handsome gorgeous – and yes, so sexy – husband-to-be, my doubts faded. Gary was The One I had been waiting for. If ever doubts reared their heads, his calming, mellifluous voice would reason them away.

The morning of our wedding arrived. Like a typically modern couple, we woke up in bed together and had our final screw as an unmarried couple.

Afterwards, as we lay there glowing, I could have murdered a post-coital cigarette. But Gary did not smoke, and out of respect for my husband I was trying to give it up (I would have a quick one later when he wasn't around).

My head was on his downy chest. "Gary?"

"Yes, Mrs Goffrey."

I purred. I liked that. "Any final doubts?" I asked.

"None, my Angel Baby. You?"

"No – none at all. But aren't you nervous or worried? Today you'll be in front of a load of my friends whom you've never met before."

"Worried? Why should I be?"

I admired his confidence. I loved him for it. I raised my head to look at his handsome face. "And you'll be meeting my Dad for the first time."

He nodded. "That's good, I've got a lot to thank him for."

True, we both had. Dad was flying over from France especially for the ceremony. Although I had money of my own from a sizeable inheritance from my grandmother, Dad's Mom, Dad had insisted that he pay for the wedding as tradition dictated. He had sent me plenty of money to pay for my wedding outfit, the ceremony, the reception, the hotel, everything. Thank you, Dad. "He's been very good to us," I said.

"I mean for you," explained Gary. "I've got to thank him for you."

Did I look like the cat with the cream, or what?

Then Gary said, "Angel Baby, I need to go back to the studio."

"Today? What on earth for?"

"Well, it's unlucky to see the bride on the morning of the wedding, isn't it?"

"How about screwing the bride on the morning of the wedding?"

"They don't say anything about that! I'll get changed there and make my way to Worth Street."

I kissed the right corner of his mouth. "Are you sure? I don't want you to be alone."

"Sure I'm sure," he licked my nose. "And anyway, I won't be alone."

"You won't?"

"No... There's always someone else there with me."

I frowned.

"I'll have my Angel Baby with me, won't I?" he smiled. "In my head." He tapped his temple. "And in my heart." He tapped his chest.

I kissed his chin. "Did I tell you that I love you?"

"Hmm..." He made a show of thinking. "You might have.

But sit on my face and tell me again!"

"My God, I'm marrying a pervert!" I laughed.

"Have I ever denied it?" He wiggled his tongue up and down lewdly.

I did what my husband requested.

16

Our wedding was a turn-up-and-go, no-appointment required ceremony at the City Clerk's Office down on Worth Street. Twenty people, mostly my friends, were there. There were just two friends of Gary, whom he said he would introduce me to but never did in the excitement of the day, and Clive who could be said to have a foot in both camps (as it were).

My wedding was beautiful (as beautiful as a civil ceremony with its conveyor-belt-like qualities can be) and, like all brides, I was The Happiest Girl In The World.

Which was ironic. Because, although I did not know it at the time, as I walked out of the building and went over to Columbus Park for a few photos, arm in arm with my husband, it was the last time I was to be happy for many, many years.

PART TWO

The darkness descends

17

The reception was at the Four Points by Sheraton, in Chelsea. It went off smoothly and everyone seemed to enjoy themselves. More people with Reception Only invitations turned up, so there were about fifty altogether. Everyone was happy for us, and even those people who spoke to me alone no longer expressed their doubts as to what I had done. No one even mentioned the fact that six weeks ago I had not even heard of Gary Goffrey. Now I was married to him.

The champagne flowed, and I had a little too much (which was becoming a habit with me). But thoughts of my husband licking the bubbly out of my belly button kept me from getting too drunk. I wanted to remember my wedding night!

Although it is a joyous occasion, I suppose every bride and groom experiences the same mixed feelings about their wedding reception: they have to stay and chat and be polite and happy, but what they really want to do is go upstairs and rip each other's clothes off.

Eventually we slipped away. The reception was still in full swing, but people understood, nudge, nudge, wink, wink, "Go easy on him, Carly", "Remember he's only human."

Finally we were alone in our room, literally The Honeymoon Suite. There was more champagne in an ice bucket on the dresser, together with a bowl of chilled strawberries. Red rose petals had been scattered in a heart shape on the bed.

"I'm going to shower," I turned back to look at my husband from the bathroom doorway. "Don't start without me."

Ten minutes later I was fresh, fragrant, and ready for my first screw as a married woman. I slid into bed next to my husband and smiled my love into his green eyes.

He pecked me on my nose, then turned away from me, leaning over his side of the bed. What was this? Did he have a surprise for me?

Yes, he did. But not what I expected.

He was fumbling with something, and then he came back up – with a computer magazine. He propped it on his lap and opened it.

What?

"Gary?" He didn't seem to hear me. Already his head was buried in an article on computer viruses or something. "Gary?" It was as if I wasn't even in the room. "Gary, what are you doing?" I laughed. This was a joke, right? I was confused.

For a full minute he did not react. Then he put his right index finger on the article to mark his place, and he turned towards me with barely concealed irritation.

"What am I doing? What does it look like I'm doing? I'm reading a magazine, Carly." And he turned back to the article as if it was the most natural thing to be doing in bed. Which I suppose it was – except for on your wedding night.

In my mind I screamed. In my mind I burst out crying. In my mind I called him every son-of-a-bitching name under the sun.

In reality I just sat there in the bed with my mouth half open, wondering if today had been the biggest mistake of my life.

Then everything was okay again. Gary finished the article, skim-read the rest of the magazine, and then threw it on the floor. He turned towards me, smiled a smile that would melt titanium, and then we made love all night long.

Well, three times anyway.

18

The next morning, Gary was going to work straight from the hotel (actually, 'work' meant that he was going back to his studio and his computer). After taking our stuff back to Barbara's, I was going apartment hunting.

Dad had given me a generous wad of fifty-dollar and one-hundred dollar bills, and I had worked out that I had enough to pay the hotel bill and still have two thousand dollars left, which might cover the deposit on an apartment without me having to dip into my money.

The hotel bill was as I expected (expensive, but worth it).

As we walked away from the Cashier I frowned as I looked in my purse. "There's five hundred dollars missing."

"Sorry, Angel Baby?"

"Gary, hold up a minute." We stopped by the main door and he turned towards me. "I should have two thousand left," I explained. "I've only got a thousand five hundred."

"Are you sure?"

"Yes, I worked it out."

"You're not wrong?"

"Not with figures, no."

"Well, you must have been a bit clumsy then. You must have dropped it on the floor as you pulled your money out. Shall we go back and look?" He made no move to go back.

"No, I haven't dropped it. All the notes were in my purse, I'd separated-out the hotel money."

"So you must have miscalculated then." He took my arm. "Come on, let's find a taxi."

I pulled away. "No, Gary, no. I don't miscalculate. Five hundred dollars is missing."

It was only a nano-second, but for a moment those piercing eyes – often so loving, always so penetrating – flashed in anger and intolerance. Then the calm amusement returned. "Carly, you're being stupid."

I felt like fighting, but what good would it do? Five hundred was missing from my purse. Had my husband taken it? I looked at his lovely, sweet, patient, understanding face. Of course he hadn't. He was right, as he always was.

I was being stupid.

Masturbate

Georgie sat hugging his knees in the corner of the studio. Daddy had left the blinds open last time he visited, and the room was now illuminated by bright, crisp December daylight.

Georgie did not want to see the light, he wanted to be kept in the dark – like he usually was. He did not like the light. In fact he hated it.

And right now he did not like Daddy either. In fact he hated him. Daddy had deliberately left the blinds open to annoy him. "Here boy, look, it's light out there. Why don't you go outside – and never come back? This is a new start for me, I wish I hadn't brought you with me. I wish I could have left you behind."

But you couldn't, could you Daddy? You were the one who took me all those years ago. You're stuck with me now, I'm never going away. Where you go, I go.

Why don't you tell her about me, Daddy? She's going to find out sooner or later. Tell her, Daddy, and let's make that new start. A ready-made family of three.

She might even love me, Daddy. Have you thought of that? She might love me. More than she loves you.

Introduce us, Daddy.

Or will I have to introduce myself?

19

Our one night at the Four Points was our honeymoon (Gary promised me a proper one when his business was up and running, he didn't want me to pay for it). Now I needed to find somewhere for us to live, quickly. It was not fair for the Married Couple to stay living with Barbara – we didn't want my friend to feel like a wallflower in her own home!

The good thing about being a make-up artist is that you meet and know a lot of people. So it was through a friend-of-a-friend that I had heard about the apartment in the Archstone up at West 54th and 10th Avenue. It was for short term lets only.

I rang Gary at the studio that afternoon. He couldn't come with me to view it – too busy, he said – but he trusted my judgement. If I thought it was right for us, we'd go for it. He would keep his studio on until we found somewhere more permanent, save him moving all his stuff and then having to move it all again.

We moved in to the Archstone two days after our wedding.

I was to move out again eight days later.

20

Three days into our marriage.

Something exciting happened at work that day. The Regional Manager visited and she announced that MAC were looking for staff for their Christopher Street shop. As one of their top artists, she asked me if I wanted to move.

I said yes straightaway. Working in a bespoke make-up shop was much better than working in a department store, and there was extra money involved too. And the icing on the cake was that my friend Jacqui would be coming with me as well.

I couldn't wait to tell Gary. He would be pleased I was getting extra money because he wasn't yet bringing anything in, and he always said he didn't like living on my inheritance. He was still spending his days in the studio on his computer, writing articles which he would electronically tout around to magazines, and also laying the foundations of his web site.

As I walked down 54th Street, I looked up at our apartment on the third floor. I could see lights on inside. Unusual. I was normally the first home. Maybe Gary had some good news too, about one of his projects, and he had come home early to tell me.

"Hi, Gary!" I called as I came through the front door.

"Hi, Angel Baby!" came his voice from behind the closed

living room door.

I went in – and stopped in my tracks.

Gary was standing in the middle of the room, legs together, feet at a quarter to three, hands cupped together in front of him at groin level. And he had no trousers on – just black socks and his black shirt.

"Hi," he said again, and lifted his hands above his head and twirled, ballerina-style. His shirt lifted to show his black pants underneath.

"Gary? What are you doing?"

"Just a little exercise, Angel Baby." He executed a rather perfect *plié*. Too perfect. "Do I look cute?"

"Strange gym outfit."

He stopped and gave me a tolerant smile. "Don't I look like something out of Matthew Bourne's Swan Lake?"

I shook my head. "Who? No, you look strange. Like a ballerina. Like you're gay." Lexington Avenue seven weeks ago flashed into my mind and then was gone, a subliminal recall.

"That's the point," he carried on with his ballet movements. "Have you never seen his Swan Lake? They're all men, that's the punchline."

"Whatever." I carried on into the room, brushing past him.

His voice did not lose the tolerance. "You're the strange one, Carly. All I'm doing is a little workout - "

"I'm moving to Christopher Street."

He did not stop his 'workout'. I expected the Black Swan to appear at any moment. Or perhaps it was already here. "To where?" he asked. *Porte de bras, demi-pointe, coupé.*

"They've asked me to go and work in the shop in Christopher Street. Near Washington Square. Jacqui's coming as well. It'll be more money."

He stopped at that. "Hey that's great, Angel Baby."

"And talking of money, what's happening with your business and projects?"

"Soon, now, soon. I've got a few meetings lined up with

potential clients. Having Clive on board helps, being able to use his name, y'know." He came over and kissed me on my forehead. I could smell his sweat. "I've been knocking out those freelance articles, so hopefully some funds will be coming in. Then I won't have to rely on you."

"How many have you sold?"

"What?"

"Articles."

"Three are doing the rounds."

"How many have you sold?"

"None. Yet. But not long now, Angel, I promise. I'll be raking it in."

21

Gary was up and out early the next morning. It seemed he could not keep away from that creepy studio of his. I just hoped his business plans and projects were going as well as he said.

I needed to leave the Archstone at nine to get to work by ten. I had paid the agents a deposit to move in, but now the rent was due, a month in advance.

I kept my checkbook in my pantie drawer (just underneath the special-occasions crotchless G-strings and the box of Tampax). Dressed and made-up, I grabbed a pen from my purse and opened the drawer, rummaging amongst my underwear.

I frowned and rummaged again, lifting out a handful of pants and the Tampax box. My hands patted the bottom of the drawer.

My checkbook wasn't there.

But I'd put it there the other day when we moved in. Where the hell was it? Had we had intruders? Had the cleaner taken it? Had it grown legs –

Just like the note I had left when I went to the hospital.

Okay, let's narrow this down. The missing note. The missing five hundred dollars. The missing checkbook. Answer this question: what's the common denominator? Not the location. Not Barbara. You've got one second to answer, ding, time's up.

The common denominator was Mr Gary Goffrey.

I couldn't believe it. I was kidding myself, reading things into things. I needed to calm down. Why would my husband take my checkbook? What for? He could get my account details but what was he going to do? Forge my signature?

I realised, of course, that there was also one other common denominator between the hospital note, the missing five hundred dollars and my checkbook.

Me.

Perhaps I had made it up about the note. Perhaps I thought I had left one but hadn't? Perhaps I had miscounted the money. Perhaps I had mislaid the checkbook?

But I distinctly remembered putting the checkbook under the Tampax. Even so, it was a long jump from a box of Tampax to accusing my husband of stealing it. What was wrong with me?

Nothing.

Because two minutes later I found my checkbook.

It was in Gary's drawer, below his shirts, tucked way at the back.

And a check was missing.

22

I probably sold two thousand bucks worth of products that day. I was busy, which was good as I didn't have time to dwell on the checkbook. But I had decided to confront Gary over dinner that night.

I was the first home and I prepared a spaghetti bolognaise, aided by a glass or two of Sicilian red from a bottle we had opened a couple of days ago.

Gary was late 'at the office' and his cellphone was going straight to voicemail – which could mean he was on his way home on the subway.

I had finished my bowl of spag bol and was enjoying a second cup of coffee when he came in. As always, I was struck by how gorgeous he looked – even if I was angry with him. There was just a slight redness around his eyes where he had been on the computer all day.

"Hi, Angel Baby." His tongue slid into my mouth. I pulled away after the kiss, resisting the urge to ask him to slide his tongue somewhere else.

"Gary, I want to talk to you."

"Dinner ready?" He looked towards the kitchen.

"Bolognaise in the saucepan. The water's boiled for your pasta."

"Great." He slid out of his leather jacket, and I admired the tanned, muscular arms beneath the T-shirt.

"Gary - "

"Yes, babe?"

"Do you know anything about my checkbook?"

"Your checkbook?" He went into the kitchen, me following. Lighting the flames beneath the saucepan, he turned towards me, frowning. "Why should I know anything about your checkbook?"

"I was looking for it - "

"Don't tell me you lost it!"

"I found it."

"Oh. Great. So what's the problem?"

"It wasn't where I put it."

"Oh?"

"It was in your shirt drawer."

He seemed not to hear me as he tipped a clump of spaghetti into the water.

"Gary!"

"What?"

"What was my checkbook doing in your drawer?"

"How should I know, Angel Baby?" He had the distracted tolerance of a parent talking to a child. "You must have put it there by mistake."

"And there's a check missing!"

"Didn't you pay the deposit by check the other day? I think you're being silly. You found your checkbook, isn't that the important thing?"

Again he made me doubt myself. His response was so reasonable.

I said lowly, sulkily, "I don't make mistakes." I'm sure he could hear the uncertainty in my voice. "I don't put things in wrong drawers. I don't miscount the money in my purse. I don't think I've written notes when I haven't - " I stopped, frozen. Then I said, "*Shit.*"

"Carly?"

"Oh shit. SHIT!" I doubled over as pain shot through my stomach. "Fuck, I need to sit down." I hobbled over to the kitchen table, clutching my tummy. A fart popped out as I sat down. "Sorry."

"The pain again?" Gary looked concerned but he stayed by the cooker, stirring the pasta. "You due on?"

"No, I - " I had to stop talking as another arrow shot through my guts. *"Christ."*

"Go and lie down baby."

I put my head down on the table. As I watched Gary straining the pasta, I said "I need the hospital."

"Haven't you got any of those tablets left?" He shook the colander and then flopped the pasta onto a plate.

"No. I – *shit!*" This was worse than last time. "I need a hospital."

"But how are you going to get there?" He was spooning on the sauce.

"What do you mean, how am I going to get there?" I croaked. "We are going to have to take a taxi."

"You want me to come with you?"

"Of course I damn well do."

"But I've just made my dinner!"

I grit my teeth. "Call me a taxi. Now."

He grinned. "You're a - "

"Don't even," I shook my head. "I will kill you where you stand."

He pulled his cellphone from his pocket. "Have you got a number?"

23

Gary made sure he ate his dinner while we waited for the taxi to arrive.

It took twenty minutes for us to get to St Vincent's and Gary hardly said a word during the journey, he was more interested in a photography book he had brought with him. Mind you, I hardly said a word either – I was more interested in dying.

The hospital was not overly busy, and I was triaged quickly. Just forty minutes later I was summoned into a cubicle, my husband in tow.

The usual examination, the prodding, the poking, the not-too-delicate parting of the lips, the internal violation. Okay, take this then go outside and sit in the corridor.

Twenty more minutes and the pain was well subsiding. We were called into an office.

As usual with the medical profession, they had discovered what was *not* wrong with me: I wasn't pregnant, there were no lumps or tumours, there didn't appear to be any muscle strain or hernia. I was not vomiting or pooing so it didn't seem to be anything I had eaten.

So what *was* wrong with me?

They didn't know.

The doctor must have spoken with us for twenty minutes. Correction. He must have spoken with me. For although he addressed many questions to us both, and one or two directly to Gary, it was me who answered.

My husband said not one word to the doctor, even when he was addressed directly. He just sat there in the room, slightly away from me, reading his book.

He was completely uninterested in anything the doctor was saying. And therefore, of course, I concluded he was completely uninterested in me also.

"What the fuck was that all about?" We were in the taxi for the ride back to the Archstone. Gary had wanted me to go to his studio, which was much nearer, but I had refused. I was in no mood to have the walls staring at me.

"What was what all about, Angel Baby?" Gary was fully attentive, loving, concerned.

"The hospital. You never said a word!"

"Oh my poor love, didn't I? I'm sorry. I told you before I was no good with hospitals. Those places give me the creeps. You shouldn't have made me go with you."

"Yes, yes, of course. It was my fault. Wanting my husband with me when I was dying."

"Now you're being dramatic."

"That's me all over, isn't it? The drama queen. I suppose you're going to say I was making it up, that you *did* talk to the doctor. Same as there wasn't money missing from my purse. Same as I didn't put my checkbook in your drawer. Same as I didn't leave a note on Barbara's coffee table."

"Angel, you're stressed."

"What should I do? See a doctor?"

"You need to rest, my love. Maybe I should go back to the studio for a few days. I can work, you can rest and get better."

I looked out of the cab window at the bright lights of 10th Avenue.

"No," I said. "I have a better idea - "

"We're here. Thanks driver, just on the left."

Gary got out as the cab came to a stop, and strolled into the building, exchanging pleasantries with the concierge who had opened the door for him. I, of course, was left to pay.

Gary hadn't asked me what my better idea was. But he would find out. Whether he wanted to or not.

Very soon.

I'll be home when?

Georgie sat hugging his knees in the corner of the studio. He was angry. So very, very angry.

All evening he had been left alone. Usually he did not mind, he was his own best friend, he could find plenty of things to amuse him.

But Daddy had said he would be home at a certain time – and he had not been. Georgie liked order. If Daddy said he was coming home, then he should come home. He should not say something and then not do it.

When Daddy had eventually turned up, he had been apologetic. So apologetic that he had not hit Georgie, like he usually did. In fact he spoke to him kindly, gently.

It had not been Daddy's fault that he had come home late. The bitch had been taken sick.

As if that wasn't bad enough, she had demanded - yes, *demanded* – that Daddy go with her to the hospital.

Why? She was the one that was ill. What could Daddy do? How *dare* she.

Now Georgie's routine was put out, and he was uncomfortable. And when he was uncomfortable he began to think those thoughts. Thoughts that Daddy had told him he should not have any more.

Think of the trouble they caused last time.

24

I left Gary the next morning. We had been married just ten days.

While Gary was in the shower I made a phone call to John, my previous boyfriend. He was dumbstruck, perplexed at hearing from me, but yes I could come and stay with him for a while if I wanted to. But wasn't I worried? What about my husband? John didn't want to be getting into any fights with some lovelorn hunk of an Aussie.

It wouldn't be like that, I assured him. This was on a strictly sleep-on-the-sofa basis only, until I had time to gather my thoughts. I just needed to get away from this man for a few days, I wouldn't even tell him I was with John.

Gary looked so handsome when he came into the kitchen for breakfast, as if he knew something was about to come down and was trying to wrong foot me. For a moment I felt my resolve weakening, but then with a deep breath I said "Gary, I'm sorry, I've made a big mistake."

He smiled as he poured himself a cup of coffee. "What's that Angel Baby? The checkbook? Don't worry about it."

"No, the mistake was marrying you."

A dramatic moment. If this was a play or a movie, Gary would freeze, the coffee still pouring into and over the rim of his cup, rolling across the table and onto the floor as he looked at me disbelievingly. Maybe he would cry, beg me to reconsider.

But things like that don't happen in real life, do they? In real life, Gary simply poured his coffee and put bread into the toaster. He had no shock reaction. Perhaps he had been expecting it.

"I'm leaving," I continued.

He spoke over his shoulder. "Are you sure that's what you want? Won't you even give us a chance?"

"I – I don't know. I need to get away. Something's not right."

"What's not right?"

"If I knew that - " I began to shout and then stopped myself.

He sipped his coffee, his back still towards me. "Where are you going?"

"Just somewhere. I'll have my cell."

Now he turned around. So handsome. So calm. "Are you sure you want to do this?"

No, I thought. "Yes," I said.

25

I stayed with John in Queens for five days. Why John? Why not Barbara or any of my other female friends? Because that would be too easy. Gary would know where to find me, and I did not want to be found. In telling Gary my history, I had exaggerated the rancour of my break-up with John, so Gary would not think of looking for me there.

John was a gentleman, as he has always been. Did I use the sofa? For the first night, yes. Did we sleep together again after that? You decide.

And I went to see Linda.

Linda was a counselor in Greenwich Village. I had been visiting her for years, when my depressions got the worst of me. She had been especially helpful when my relationship with John was coming to an end.

Her most valuable trait? She listened to me.

"I've married this man and I don't know what to do," I was sitting on the easy chair in her quiet, cosy consulting room, one leg up underneath me. "I think he's lying to me." I told her all about how I had met Gary, how I had fallen in love, and then the 'little incidents' of the note, the money and the checkbook. And why was I getting these pains in my stomach?

One thing about Linda, she was a professional. Never had she told me something just because she thought I wanted to hear it. She didn't now.

After I had finished my story, she sat back in her chair, tapping her pencil against her chin as she studied me. Eventually she said, "Old maxims aren't always right, you know Carly."

"Maxims?"

"Marry in haste, repent at leisure? Don't believe it, it doesn't have to be like that. To me, Gary sounds like a lovely guy. He's new to the country. Trying to find his feet. He's met you and fallen in love. He's so nice and calm with you, and you're not used to things being like that. You might be trying to find fault where there is none. Yes, the checkbook and those other things, I don't understand. But there is a rational explanation for each of them. Are you over-analysing?"

I looked at her, but in my mind I was seeing this poor innocent guy from Australia who was getting all this weird stuff from me because – let's face it – I was a manic depressive. Christ, what had I done? What had I done in marrying him? What had I done in leaving him?

"You think so?" I asked.

"Do *you* think so?"

"...Maybe. But what about the pains in my stomach?"

"Anxiety? Stress?"

"Oh God." We were quiet for a minute. Then I asked, "Should I go back?"

"Only you can decide that, Carly."

"I just don't know what to do - "

At that moment my purse on the table next to me started to buzz. Shit, I hadn't turned my cell off!

Linda nodded. "It doesn't matter, go ahead."

I took the phone out of my bag and looked at the screen.

With a timing that was almost mystical in its perfection, Mr Gary Goffrey without a D, my husband, the man I loved, was calling me.

∞

I called him back fifteen minutes later as I left Linda's office and walked north up Thompson Street for some retail therapy in the area's eclectic mix of boutiques.

"Hi Gary, it's me."

"Angel Baby, how are you? You all right? I've been thinking about you. Truth be told, I haven't stopped thinking about you."

Nor me you. "Gary – "

"You know, I completely understand how you must be feeling. Here we are married, man and wife, and we haven't even known each other for two months yet!"

"Have you had any doubts?"

"Doubts? No. I'm crazy about you, Carly."

"We don't even know each other very well. Were we foolish?"

"Nah. Impetuous, maybe. But what's life if you can't be impetuous?" He was quiet for a moment, then said, "Angel Baby, I'd love you to come home."

Walking along, phone to my ear, in the grey cold of New York, I began to cry gently. "I'm scared, Gary. Scared I've made a very big mistake. I don't know how to read you. It's me, I know it's me. Maybe I'm not meant for relationships, let alone marriage."

"That's why it's perhaps good that we did it quickly. But I quite understand. You stay away as long as you need. If you want to meet somewhere, we can. It's up to you. It's going to be okay."

All my life I'd wanted to hear those words: *it's going to be okay*. No more punishment in the Wendy House, no more being the child nobody wanted around. Thinking of what Linda had said, hearing my husband being so kind, so understanding, I began to wonder: what was wrong with me?

"Oh Gary," I said. "You can't begin to know how much in love with you I am."

"Come home, Angel Baby."

Five days after walking out on my marriage, I went back to Gary.

And to three years of unimaginable hell.

The damage is done

Georgie sat hugging his knees in the corner of the studio. His gaze was wistful.

Do you think she'll come back, Daddy? Are you sure? You seem very confident –

No, no, please don't hit me! I don't doubt you. I trust you.

When she comes back, will you keep your promise, Daddy? Will you introduce me to her? I bet she can't guess who I am!

I know, I know! The other times, it was my fault. I damaged your relationships. I was bad, so very, very bad. But not this time. This time I will be good. This time I will be very good.

This time she'll hardly know I'm there. It'll just be our cosy little family of three. This time I will be careful, I promise.

Can I play with her, Daddy?

"Do you want to stop for a bit?" asked Marinelli.

I was aware that my hands were clenched tight together. Marinelli had noticed it too.

"Perhaps another tea?" I suggested.

"Sure."

"But let's not stop. I must do this now I've started. Do you mind if I smoke in here?" I held up my packet of Marlborough.

"Usually you have to go outside – but in your case we'll make an exception."

"Thanks." I lit up.

Swallowing the wonderful, calming smoke, I said "That was the beginning. Now I'll tell you things as I remember them. They didn't all happen at once, they happened over the three years of my marriage, so I might jump about a bit. You might not believe some of the things I am about to tell you…"

I paused to let Marinelli reassure me, but there was no reaction.

"…But they are all true."

I took a deep breath and continued.

PART THREE

Vignettes of my life

26

As soon as I went back into the Archstone, I had a bad feeling. It was not the feeling I used to get in Gary's studio, where I thought the walls were watching me, it was just a feeling of *I don't want to be here.*

Now that was interesting. *I don't want to be here.* Not *I don't want to be with Gary.* I resolved that one of the first things we would do was to find a new place, somewhere permanent, not a short term let. Somewhere for us *both.* Somewhere big enough so that Gary could give up his creepy studio and he could work on his articles and his burgeoning business from home. *Our* home.

Gary must have sensed my unease as I walked through the front door. He put my bags down in the hallway, turned, kissed me (more please), and said "Let's go for a walk."

"What?"

"I can tell you're uneasy, Angel Baby. Let's go for a nice long walk for the afternoon and talk. I've been exploring while you've been away. I'm going to take you to one of my favorite places."

I smiled at my husband. That was considerate, trying to make me feel at ease. "Okay. Where is it?"

"Ah, that would be telling. It's a secret. I'm just going to take you there."

I kissed him on the cheek. "Then let's go." I felt happy. At last I had made a right decision. I vowed that this marriage was going to work.

Gary was true to his word. We did walk. In New York, of course, you can walk straight. North or south, east or west, but primarily straight. We walked south. For the afternoon. For three hours. Straight down Broadway. Now, I love my adopted city but *Hello?*

On and on we walked, Gary refusing to be drawn on where we were going. It was cold, but after hitting the wall with the initial calf-strain, I have to say it was not unenjoyable. In the high heat of a New York summer it would have been different, indeed not doable.

My feet began to ache as we passed City Hall. But the pleasure of the walk did not pall as I now knew where we were going. Or I thought I did.

"It's Ground Zero, isn't it?" I said smiling. Clever girl.

"What is?"

"Where we're going."

"Is it, Angel Baby? I don't think so. Why would that be anybody's favourite place?"

The smile dropped from my face. I felt stupid.

We passed Ground Zero a block to our right (I still can't believe those towers are not there), crossed over Liberty Street and continued on. We crossed over Wall Street on our left (that had been my next guess, but I didn't say anything), and then taking my elbow Gary steered me across the road into Trinity Churchyard.

I presumed we were taking a short cut through to the mysterious favorite place, but halfway in Gary stopped walking, his arm around me. We were well away from the road. Around us, the tombs and skeletal trees matched the dour mood of the grey sky above. We stopped by the Firemen's Monument.

"What do you think?" he asked.

I looked up at him. "What do I think what?"

"This is it. My favorite place."

"A cemetery?"

"Can't you see the beauty here?"

I admit that many people had, and still do. But I couldn't. "No, not really."

Gary did not alter his grip on me at all, but suddenly the arm around my shoulders felt like it had changed from a loving embrace to a restraint.

"Dead people, Carly. Where they are now, we will be, and all that. What lovely graves. You won't see these styles in any other New York cemetery. Let's see who died here!"

I thought of pointing out that probably none of them had died here, they had died elsewhere and had been brought here, but my husband was so enthusiastic, dragging me behind him from tomb to tomb, saying their names out loud, that I didn't have the heart to ruin the afternoon with pedantry. *Alexander Hamilton, Robert Fulton, John Jacob Astor...*

He was so keen, so eager, as we passed between the tombs. He almost skipped along.

Like a little boy.

27

When I determine to do something, when I promise to do something, I do it. Again using contacts (this time, surprisingly, one recommended by Gary), I managed to find us an apartment in an old but refurbished town house down on Minetta Lane, just south of Washington Square Park. I liked the place immediately I saw it. It was big enough for the both of us and then some, and it was in a part of New York I was familiar with. And there was an added bonus that Gary's spooky studio was nearby, so we could move his things quickly and easily. Instantly I felt much happier.

The house consisted of five storeys plus a basement cellar. Ours was the middle apartment, on the third floor. Again Gary didn't come to see it beforehand, he left everything to me ("I trust your judgement, Angel Baby."). But soon he was once and for ever clearing his things out of his studio, storing a lot of the unnecessary stuff in the musty old cellar of the new house, which, for some reason the agent never explained, 'came with' our apartment.

The apartment was fully furnished, and on the day we moved in I cleaned absolutely everything. Cupboards, floors, walls, you name it. I saw every nook and cranny of the place, I knew for certain that all cupboards and drawers and any other storage area (or area of concealment) were empty.

Why am I telling you this little detail?

You'll find out.

As I did.

28

Immediately upon moving in, I felt much happier. Happier about myself, happier about Gary, happier about my marriage. This time I was determined to make a go of it. I was a sane, grown-up woman. I had made a conscious choice to marry this guy, I should make a go of it. And there was no evidence that he had anything to do with The Little Incidences; the note, the money, the checkbook could all have been pernicious circumstances into which I read things that were just not there.

I liked Gary, I loved Gary, but I didn't know Gary. Therefore, I reasoned, I must get to know him. Like women who had arranged marriages, I must get to know my husband after the vows had been taken.

We were both busy in the first year of living there. I left MAC to concentrate on my true calling of being a freelance make-up artist. I was running around like the proverbial blue-assed fly, working on my portfolio, going to see agents, getting my career sorted out. And I did well. Slowly, gradually, my client base grew. I became known by the most powerful recommendation in the world: word of mouth. I worked steadily, mixing private one-on-one jobs with fashion shoots and TV and movie work.

Gary was busy writing articles and reviewing books from publishers and the like, and slowly constructing his web site. Mainly he worked from home, at the workstation he had set up by the window in our front room, overlooking Minetta Lane below. Clive would phone often, and they were exchanging e-mails regularly.

To the outside world we must have seemed like the archetypal yuppies, a successful couple ruled by their BlackBerries, who would even have to make appointments to have sex ("Can you fit me in on Monday?"). In reality things were not as rigid (sorry!) as that, but we were two people living together joined by the fact that we were married. But we were not A Couple.

But, like that woman with the arranged marriage, I did slowly get to know Gary. Little pieces of his personality emerged, like the slow drip of a tap that you don't hear at first but when you become aware of it you can hear nothing else... until it takes up your life, filling it completely until that's all you are aware of. Even though your 'normal' life goes on, you become consumed by the dripping which, although it hasn't changed in frequency or volume from that first drip which you didn't even notice, now consumes you.

And drives you mad.

29

Gary could be very forgetful – or at least I thought so at the time. I would go to work, come home and, as usual, he would be on his computer. He was in the apartment on his own during the day and for safety's sake he would lock our front door and leave the key in the lock on the inside. Which meant, of course, that I couldn't get my key in from the outside.

Although I admired his sense of security, not being able to get into my own home irritated me. I'd even call him beforehand to tell him I was on my way and to take the key out of the door – but no, it would still be in there when I got home and I would have to knock.

Gary's response to my irritation would be, "Oh yeh, yeh, sorry, I keep forgetting." And, dozy little moppet that I was, I used to accept this. I regarded Gary as highly intelligent, always on the computer, reading computer books, teaching himself programming, designing his web library and such, and I could see that he was so engrossed in his work that he would forget to remove the key.

It was a simple little thing. One of the drips of the tap. It was no harm really. He would just have to let me in each day.

So what was my problem?

My problem was that for the three years of our marriage, if my husband was indoors and working on his computer, not once could I get into my own home without having to knock on my door to ask him to let me in.

30

I wasn't working that day, so I had been down to the shops on MacDougal Street to get some milk and bread. Post was on the mat when I came back to the house. I sorted out envelopes for the other residents and left them in their boxes. There were a couple of magazine-subscription type gaudy letters for Gary and a plain brown envelope addressed to me. It just reeked 'Official'. Probably a tax bill which I would divert immediately to my accountant.

Gary was still in bed so I was able to get into the apartment. I put coffee on, put some bread in the toaster, and opened the envelope.

It was from the Immigration Service. They wanted to ensure that I was married to and living with Mr G Goffrey. Authentication was required. I could either present myself personally to 26 Federal Plaza or send my evidence to them by registered mail.

Gary was indifferent when I told him, after all they wanted to see me not him. So to save any loss, I took myself and my evidence (passport, utility bills, marriage certificate, Gary's Social Security details, etc) off to Federal Plaza for interview. What an experience that was, I can tell you. Why did I come out feeling like I was the Mastermind behind some huge immigration racket?

In reality, they accepted my evidence but they said they would check with me in eighteen months time before finally 'submitting' my husband for residency.

What am I to you?

Georgie stood in the middle of the studio. Try as he might, he could not stop a tear rolling down his left cheek. His head felt sore where Daddy had hit him when he had appeared this morning.

This is it, boy. We're out of this stinking place forever. What? You like it here? Don't start with me, lad. You wanted out of here as much as I did. And now we have somewhere.

And someone.

What am I to you, Daddy?

What are you to me, boy? A fucking hindrance, that's what you are. The bane of my life. I should have left you behind in Australia. God knows, I tried. But I come over to this country, I turn around – and there you are! Shit, now don't you start that crying!

I – I'm just scared, Daddy. Scared that you'll leave me. Scared that you love her more than you love me.

Don't be silly now, boy, don't be silly. How could I love anyone more than you? Heck, I've even got somewhere special you can live in this new house. Somewhere just for you. You can stay in there and I'll come to see you every day.

And then sometime, when the time is right, you can come up and meet your new Mommy. Won't that be nice? Sometime when everything is settled. Won't she be surprised! But we have to time it right. One night, when it's dark…

I love you, Daddy. Let's go to our new home.

31

Finally all Gary's stuff was moved in. It had taken him what I thought was an unnecessarily long time, but at last he had given up the creepy studio and handed back the keys.

He let me back into the apartment as usual that evening, and as soon as I entered the living room I saw a new occupant sitting on the couch.

So who was this?

Gary had entered the room behind me, and I could feel the anticipation coming off him. Obviously he wanted me to say something. I obliged. "Who's this then?"

He pretended nonchalance. "That? That's Teddy." He picked up the toy, the new occupant. "Teddy's been with me all my life. Where I go, he goes. Teddy knows everything. Teddy is the only one I can trust. He's been in the studio until now."

I looked at him to see if he was joking. His face was whimsical, far away.

"So why haven't you given teddy a name?"

"I have. He's Teddy."

"So is Teddy a boy or a girl?"

He just looked at me. His eyes had changed, subtly but definitely, from the dreamy look to something more scheming. Something *amused*. And I knew then that the game was on.

I said, "You can't remember whether Teddy's a boy or a

girl?"

"It's just Teddy."

"Well, obviously we don't want Teddy in the marriage, do we? Why don't you just put him back in the box and put it in the cellar?"

"No, no," his smile was cold. "Teddy is my friend. He stays out."

Later, when I went into the bedroom, there was Teddy in the middle of the pillows.

And for the remainder of our marriage, Teddy was always somewhere.

The next evening, there was a brightly-wrapped box on the table in the living room. Gary had greeted me enthusiastically when he opened the door, a loving, lustful, tongue-filled kiss which augured well for sex later. "Hi, Angel Baby," he grinned.

"What's this?" I asked, pointing to the box.

"For you."

I picked it up.

"Just something to tell you I love you."

Mm, nice words always made my lips tingle. "Can I open it?"

"Of course."

I pulled off the paper to reveal a shoe box. Had he bought me Jimmy Choo's? I smiled over to him.

"Open it then," he nodded.

I put the box down on the table and took off the lid.

Inside was a bed of white silk. And lying on the bed of silk was a teddy bear.

"I thought you would like one too," he enthused.

"Th – thanks, Gary."

"What are you going to call it?"

I could not keep the sharpness out of my voice. "I don't know what to call it. Because I don't know what sex it is. We can't have two of the same sex, can we? So I'm going to presume your's is a boy and mine is a girl. I'll call mine Minnie Teddy.

Okay?"

"So there we are, a complete family." He came over and put his arms around me from behind. "All fi- four of us. Isn't this nice?"

Nice was the last thing it was. Weird, maybe. Nice, no.

Things were very stilted for the rest of the evening, at least from my side. Gary seemed not to know that anything was wrong. We still had sex that night – but we weren't the only ones.

"You coming to bed?" I finished my second glass of red wine as the weather girl (sorry, weather *person*) on NBC was predicting mild things for tomorrow and, for some reason, was going on in great detail about the weather we had already had that day (why do they do that?).

"I'll be there in a minute, Angel Baby. Just finishing up here."

Up and here was the computer, of course.

I had a pee, had a little wash down in anticipation, and walked naked into the bedroom.

On the bed, Minnie Teddy was on all fours and Teddy was positioned behind her, doggie-style.

Oh for God's sake –

Suddenly, I was shoved from behind, and I fell forward onto the bed. I hadn't heard Gary approach. I fell onto my knees and made the bears bounce apart. Then Gary's hands were on my bottom and I could feel the denim of his jeans against me, then the cold of his zip and the warmth of his flesh as he got his dick out.

"Hello Little Girl," he leered. "Fancy a foursome?"

32

That wasn't the only 'Little Girl' incident.

We carried on with our lives. My freelance work was erratic, so I went back to MAC for the steady wage, freelancing for extras when I could. Gary continued to write his articles from home, and occasionally he would do temp work at publishing houses. People would ask me how my marriage was, and I would reply with the usual platitudes. When I was saying "Great," "Fine," I really wanted to be saying "I'm worried. He's a strange man. I'm not at all sure of him." But if I said that, people would ask me why. And when I heard myself voicing my doubts, trying to explain The Little Incidences, it all sounded so pathetic, as if I was a woman looking for an excuse not to like my husband, not to make my marriage work.

One day we were walking along 6th Avenue together. We had reached an art shop and at first I was too busy looking in the window to notice that he was no longer with me. Then I looked back. Gary was stationary ten feet behind me. He had the silliest little smile on his face, like the smile of a small boy. The green eyes were sparkling.

"Gary?" I frowned.

Instantly the smile changed as he arched his right eyebrow and pursed his lips lasciviously. "Oh, hello little girl," he said. "You look very cute. Would you come home with me?"

"Gary!" I grabbed his arm, gritting my teeth and speaking lowly. "Fucking pack it up. I'm your wife, for God's sake. I'm not a little girl. People are looking."

He giggled - a horrible, haunting sound. "Okay, Mommy. Whatever you say."

33

Gary loved cats – as I did – and we had discussed getting one. Yes, I know, the child substitute and all that. I've never looked at cats that way, to me they are just pets. But I had resolved already that there was no way I was going to have children with Gary, so maybe the age-old theory was right.

But whereas I simply liked cats, Gary, as in most things he did, could become obsessive. Once we had spoken about it, he took it for granted that we would be getting one. One evening, out of the blue, he began to rock his arms as if he was holding a baby, humming a little tune.

"Gary, what are you doing?" I asked.

"I'm holding Lychee."

"Who's Lychee?"

"One of the cats I had in Australia." He blew a gentle kiss at the empty space in his arms. "Oh my little Lychee, I love you so much." The tears welled in his eyes, and he looked to a point somewhere far outside our living room.

Then, as quickly as they had come, the tears dried and his face went cold. He said, "But he died. All my cats died."

"All of them?"

"Yes, all of them."

"How many?"

"Four all together."

"How did they die?"

He shrugged. "I don't know, they just died." And then that was it, over. "Glass of red wine, Carly?" he asked.

We never did get a cat.

34

It was the morning after the 'dying cats' revelations of the night before. Just five seconds after I woke up, the stomach pains started. *Shit, here we go again.*

At least this time I was nearer to St Vincent's.

Over the coming months, I was a regular client. Although it always started off with the most severe stomach pains, I had differing follow-on symptoms. Sometimes there were just the stomach cramps, often lots of vomiting. One time I even had blurred eyesight. I was given many and various diagnoses. There seemed to be a different one for each time I went: urine problems, upset kidneys, something intolerance. I was told to lay off the red wine.

And every single time I went to the hospital I had the same rigmarole with Gary.

"Are you coming with me?"

"Oh, do I have to?"

Shouting from me.

Sighing from him.

"Oh, okay," And he would take the inevitable book with him and say not one word to the hospital staff.

35

Books would filter into the apartment from publishing companies, for Gary to preview, review, whatever. He also received lots of computer disks from various potential clients for his web library. He was always writing. Always on his computer.

We hardly ever went out – so imagine my surprise one day when he said to me "David Bailey's got an exhibition on."

"Oh yeh?" I was watching *What Not To Wear* on TV.

"At Soho Photo Gallery in TriBeCa, White Street. I did some work for them, a couple of brochures ago. I bet I can get some tickets for the opening. Fancy going?"

My God, my husband was actually going to take me out! Before I could answer, he asked "You do know who David Bailey is? The photographer?"

"Of course I know who he is. Actually I used to nanny for somebody who was very good friends with David Bailey. On occasions either the Bailey's kids would come over or my boss's kids would go over to theirs."

"Wow. Right, I'll give the Gallery a ring."

The opening was in a week's time. Gary pulled his strings, and our invitation to the opening came in the post two days later. Actually, I say 'our' invitation – it was an invitation for Mr Gary Goffrey and Guest. I knew my place.

It was a laid-back, stroll in stroll out affair, and naturally David Bailey was the centre of attention. It took two hours before even the charming Gary could manoeuvre his way over to talk to him. Mr Goffrey's guest tagged along in his slipstream.

Gary and David talked about photography (surprise!) for a few minutes, Gary explaining who he was, what he'd done et cetera, and then he said almost as an afterthought, "Oh, this is my wife Carly."

I shook David's hand. "Hello."

"Hello." (What is it about British accents?)

"But you know her, don't you?" said Gary. "She used to nanny for you, used to look after your kids."

There was a silence. I couldn't believe what I'd just heard. Oh earth, please open up and take me right now.

The earth was saved its job by someone coming over for their turn with the maestro. David turned away.

I grabbed Gary by the arm. "What the fuck did you say that for?" I growled softly.

He was all innocence. "What, Angel Baby? You told me you used to work for him."

"No I did not. I said I used to work for somebody who knew him. I saw his kids. I never saw him."

"That's not what you told me, Angel Baby."

"Yes, I did." Didn't I? "I feel fucking embarrassed. I want to go."

"Not yet, we haven't seen everyone yet. Contacts, networking, you know. And don't be embarrassed, Carly," Gary began to walk away from me. "He's probably forgotten about you already."

36

"I've bought my little girl a present."

The 'little girl' appellation grated like nails on a blackboard, but I was used to it by now. I tried to be pleasant, but a particularly busy day in MAC had added to my already constant feeling of tiredness. It was the day after the David Bailey embarrassment.

"What have you done that for?" I threw my purse down onto the couch and took off my coat.

"Can't I buy my little girl a present? To let her know her Daddy loves her. And to say sorry for the mix-up at the gallery."

So it was a mix-up, was it? Not my fault after all? "I don't need a present, Gary."

It was as if he didn't hear me. "Do you remember that kitchenware shop we went to a few months ago? Lamalle's? I went back there today."

"You've been out of the house two days running? All the way to West 25th!" My sarcasm fell on stony ground.

"It's inside." He grabbed my hand. I was dragged into the kitchen. Oh great, I thought, he's bought me a saucepan.

Sitting on the work surface was a slim box. He gestured to it. "For you, Angel Baby."

I picked it up, and I have to admit the packaging spelt class. I took off the lid. Inside, on a bed of white silk, was an ugly, stainless steel cleaver.

"It's a Japanese bone chopping knife!" he enthused.

For a while, I said nothing. Then I asked, "What have you bought that for?"

"I thought you'd like it. Isn't it beautiful? It's brilliant at crushing garlic."

Okay. "But wouldn't one use a garlic crusher?"

"No, no, you put the garlic underneath and you just slam it."

"I see."

"And, of course, it chops clean through bone. No messing about. Straight through with one blow."

I stared at him. The little boy was looking back at me, the green eyes shining and alive – which was better than I felt at that time. Eventually I sighed. "Thank you, Gary. Thank you."

And back he went to his computer, as contented as a praised child.

37

"You're such a lazy bastard, do you know that?" I shouted from the kitchen. It had been a long day: a half day off from MAC and an advertising photoshoot in the afternoon that hadn't finished until 22:00. "Why don't you do some washing while I'm out working my ass off twenty hours a day, seven days a week?"

"Oh, I'm sorry - "

"No, no, that's all right, you stay on the computer."

"I meant to do some, but I forgot."

"Yeh, like you forget everything, Gary. Don't worry, I'll do it."

So our washing machine was thundering around at midnight. God knows what the neighbours must have thought, but they never said anything. They probably thought the husband and wife were involved in some energetic lovemaking. Banging. Literally!

But I knew, I just *knew*, what would happen the next day, and I wasn't disappointed.

I came home at a normal hour, and there was the picture of domestic bliss: husband working away on his computer, the smell of a freshly-cooked jambalaya coming from the kitchen, and the washing machine just coming to the end of its cycle. It was uncanny timing how the machine was on its final spin as

Gary opened the front door for me.

We exchanged platitudes and I went and had a ten minute shower. Tired but clean, I dressed in my comfies and went into the kitchen to get my food (credit where it was due, Gary was a good cook - when he could be bothered). The washing cycle had finished but the clothes were still in the machine.

I took a breath to say something, and then decided not to. What would be the point? It was his stuff (mine was washed last night), but I would do the wifely thing and hang it up for him.

In amongst his clothes I found my long woolly black pantyhose and seven pairs of my G-strings.

"Excuse me," I called, "but what on earth are my pantyhose doing in the washing machine?"

No reply. I went and stood in the living room doorway. "Gary?"

With a click of his mouse to change the screen, he turned around from his computer. "Yes, Angel Baby?"

"I asked you what my pantyhose were doing in the washing machine. I haven't worn them – and before you try to convince me that I have, I haven't, okay?"

"Ah." He didn't look as sheepish as I had expected him to. "Yeh, well, it was freezing here the other day. It is the middle of winter. I was sat here and I couldn't warm up, so I thought what is there in this house that I can use? So I borrowed your tights."

"And my pants, Gary?"

"Yeh, well, when I was in Australia I used to wear these boxer shorts? And I used to get these irritations? So the doctor gave me some cream and antibiotics for this rash I used to get, and the doctor said I was not to wear anything that would restrict me around this area and make me sweaty, so the best thing was to wear a G-string."

Hmm. Lucky me, I had married the only guy in the world who was told to wear a G-string on medical advice! I wish I could have talked to that doctor. "If you're cold, I'll buy you some long johns in Bloomie's."

"No, Angel Baby, they'll make me itch... I like the fabric of yours."

"Then go buy your own, Gary," I said tightly. "And keep your cock out of my pants."

38

This was ridiculous. Wearing my pantyhose was one thing – his excuse, as ever, was reasonable - but wearing my G-string pants? I think not.

Things flashed back into my mind: our first date, when I was waiting for him outside Bloomingdale's and I saw what I thought was a gay man waiting further along the road; his little ballerina posing, using the excuse of exercising; the times when he behaved like a naughty little boy...

This was something that I couldn't let rest, which I couldn't brush off as being 'just his way'. Was he gay? Certainly not completely, he was very good in bed. Bi, then?

And there was another question to ask: why did he marry me if his orientation went in another direction?

Wearing my underwear became a regular occurrence with him. Now it was out in the open, it didn't seem to worry him; in fact he became more brazen, more open about it, despite my protestations. And no, he never did buy his own.

I tried to ask him about it one evening over dinner. "Gary, it's not really normal, you know, you wearing my underwear."

He smiled his little boy smile but said nothing.

"I married a man and I think it should stay that way," I continued. "If you've got something to tell me, I think you should tell me."

The smile dropped from his face. He glared. "I've got nothing to tell you."

I returned the glare. "That's you all over, isn't it? Nothing to tell me. You never tell me anything. I know only the minimum about you, and that's only what I've forced out of you."

He sighed. "I've told you about my life in Australia. What else do you want to know?"

"Pick any personal subject. Your parents. You only told me the minimum about them."

"So?"

"So?! I'm your wife, dammit. I'm entitled to know about my husband. I'm entitled to know everything."

"My Mom's a cow, my Dad's dead. Satisfied?" He was on the verge of shouting. I seemed to have wandered into sore point territory, but I wasn't going to let go. This bastard was going to talk to me.

"When did your dad die?"

"Can't remember."

"You can't remember when your Dad died? You must."

"Nope."

"How old were you when he died?"

"Er... Twenty."

"And how old are you now?"

"Thirty-two."

"Right, so twelve years ago. There, now we're getting somewhere." If he wanted to be treated like a child, then I would treat him like one.

"Where did he die?"

"Can't remember."

"At home?"

"Can't remember."

"I think you can remember, Gary. Stop the bullshit. Did he die at home, perhaps?"

"Yeh, he did."

"Do you know what he died of?"

"No. He just died."

"Did you talk to him before he died?"

"No."

"Well, normally people do. To say goodbye or something."

"Actually, he talked to me."

"What did he say to you?"

"He said sorry."

That surprised me. "Pardon?"

"He said sorry."

"Why would your father say sorry? For what?"

"I dunno."

Was I on to something here? "Did he do something to you, perhaps?"

The green eyes were like ice. "I don't know what you're talking about."

"I think you do, Gary. Is there something you're not telling me?"

"For fuck's sake, Carly. What is this, a bloody psychiatric examination?"

"If you want it to be. Obviously something has happened to you in the past, because you wouldn't behave the way you do. Maybe at some stage in your life, without you wanting to perhaps, maybe you've been with a man, and you quite liked it or something like that?"

"No, no, no, no, NO!" He thumped his fist on the table with each denial.

And with that, the normally scarily placid Gary Goffrey picked up the solid wood kitchen table and flung it across the room.

39

Things were never the same after that. Sure, he instantly apologised for throwing the table, but as the days, weeks, months went on, things just got weirder and weirder. It was like I had partially opened a door in the disturbed psyche of Gary Goffrey without a D, and the demons within would take it in turns to come out.

He had always been obsessive about cleanliness, but now he progressed to washing the bathroom and kitchen down with alcohol daily.

The cleanliness obsession extended to me.

"You're not going to work like that, are you?" He was standing by the front door.

I was already running late, and I was in no mood for this. "Yes," I looked down at my black top and black skirt. "What's wrong with it?"

"Oh no, my Angel Baby." He ran from the room like a concerned, helpful little boy, returning with a clothes brush. "Right, turn around."

"What are you doing?"

"I'm cleaning you. If MAC insist you wear black then you must be spotless."

He tried to straighten my shoulders and my waist. I shrugged him off. "Gary! Just piss off, will you? Leave me alone."

"Okay… But there's just a little bit there - "

I slapped his hand. "Well, it can fucking stay there."

I slammed the apartment door and stomped down the stairs.

When I was outside in the street, I told myself not to look up. Don't do it, Carly, you'll know what you'll see. But Carly did do it.

And there he was, as he was every day, in the living room window, like a little lost orphan left at home, a small, sad little smile on his face, his left hand slowly waving goodbye, back and forth, hypnotically…

Some evenings, in fact, as many evenings as I could, I went out with friends. Gary would ask me where I was going, but I would not tell him.

One evening, after I had been round Barbara's for a few hours, a few glasses of white wine and a few smokes, I was coming up the stairs at West 4th Street Station when I was aware of someone close behind me. Every New Yorker's nightmare. My hand tightened on my purse, and I felt in my pocket for my keys to use as a weapon.

"Carly?" said a familiar voice.

I stopped at the top of the steps and turned round. Gary was standing behind me. "Gary?"

"Hello."

"I didn't know you were going out tonight."

"Well, seeing as you went out I thought I would to. Fancy us bumping into each other on our way back. How mad's that?"

How mad indeed. And how mad would it be if I just raised my leg now and kicked you straight back down those stairs?

I didn't, of course.

Do I sound like a miserable bitch? A miserable bitch who found her Mister Right and then used every opportunity to pick out his bad points? Did he have bad points?

I *wanted* to make my marriage work. That's why I stuck at it for so long. Perhaps all this stuff was normal when two people were married, when two people were in love. How should I know?

Perhaps there weren't any head games going on. Everything that happened in that first year could be put down to mistake or misunderstanding. There was not one thing where an impartial observer could say *Gary did this deliberately*.

Which meant one of two things.

Either I was wrong: the girl who grew up without ever knowing what love was and therefore could not recognise it when it came along, shunning it as something alien to be feared.

Gary was a very, very clever manipulative psycho.

By now, after twelve months, I was totally uncomfortable with Gary's character. I simply could not get on his wavelength. I could not gel with him. So I kept myself busy. I was still at MAC, but the freelance work had picked up again.

My life at that time consisted of going to work, seeing friends (who kept me sane), being ill, and being married to this weirdo. That was my lot. I had made my bed.

I was prepared to cut Gary as much slack as he wanted, but I was thinking *One day, I'm out of here. I don't know how or when, but one day this marriage is going to end.*

40

I was in a good mood that evening. The next day was my day off and I was going to meet my friends Jacqui and Tracy for a girls' afternoon. I would give them a call in the morning and we would make arrangements to meet.

I ate some chicken creole which Gary had prepared (delicious, as always), had just one glass of wine, and then, quite abruptly, I felt drained. It was all I could do to take my make-up off, and I crawled into bed at nine. Obviously I had been working too hard, that's why I was so tired. But at least I could sleep late the next morning, then meet Jacqui and Tracy at one. It will be fantastic, I said to myself. And I will be away from the apartment and from Gary.

Suddenly I was aware of Gary stroking my hair. I hadn't heard him come into the bedroom. I looked up at him smiling down at me and then I closed my eyes again.

And then I jumped and was awake again. Gary was not there. I hadn't felt like I'd been asleep – I hadn't felt anything – but the bedside clock said six. Gary was not beside me. What was he doing up already? He never usually surfaced before nine at the earliest.

"Gary?" I propped myself up on my elbows. "Gary!" I reached for the water glass on the bedside table, but it was empty. I was still frowning in confusion when he appeared in the doorway. "Wh – what are you doing up?" I asked.

The smile was open and innocent. "I'm on the computer."

"But it's six in the morning!"

He skipped over to the bed. Oh Christ, don't tell me he was in little boy mode. "No, my Angel Baby, don't be silly. It's not six in the morning, it's six o'clock at night."

"*What?*"

"My Angel Baby, you're just tired, aren't you?"

I couldn't grasp it. Six o'clock at *night*?

"But... I was supposed to meet some friends for lunch. Did they call?"

"No, no one's called."

Strange, but I didn't have the strength to argue. "Oh, okay. I..." I flopped back onto my pillows. "I think I'll just stay here for a while."

"Okay, my Angel Baby. I'm going back to work."

On my own, I was confused and not a little frightened. Had I slept for twenty-one hours? And I was embarrassed. Jacqui and Tracy would be really pissed off with me. I didn't want to phone them now and say sorry I didn't meet up with you, I slept through the day. How pathetic would that sound?

Twenty-one hours of pee was telling me it wanted to be released, so I forced myself out of bed. I knew where the bedroom door was, but my legs didn't seem to. I found myself walking in a zigzag fashion across the room, as if I was a crab trying to avoid a sniper's bullet.

Coming back from the john, I looked into the living room, holding tightly on to the doorframe. Gary was aware of this naked zombie standing there, and he looked over. Then he nodded at the floor. I looked down. Next to the door he had laid out several pairs of his shoes.

"Angel, I'm busy on here. Would you mind polishing those for me? I particularly like the underneath bit polished."

What? I looked at the shoes, undulating with the floor. "Not now, Gary," I said. "Maybe another day. I feel like shit. Sorry, I have to go back to bed."

I had work on a shoot the next day. I managed to get up and get there on time, but I couldn't focus, I couldn't see what I was doing. Naturally I couldn't tell this to anybody. But nobody seemed to notice, my work was praised as always.

Back home that evening, I told Gary that I had problems with my eyes. He was sympathy itself. "It will be okay, Angel Baby." He patted my hair as he looked into my eyes. "Get yourself to an optician tomorrow. I just love your beautiful green eyes."

I frowned through my haze. "What do you mean, green? I have blue eyes."

"No, they're like mine, they're green."

"They're not, Gary." I stumbled into the bathroom. I called out, "My eyes have always been - " I stopped.

I might not be able to focus properly, but looking back at me from the mirror were… two green eyes.

My eyes had changed color.

41

There was never a dull moment with Gary – and I don't mean that in the nice sense.

It was two weeks later. My eyes had reverted to their normal blue, coinciding with a notable upturn in my health. I still didn't feel right, but I felt a lot better than I had been. Grateful for small mercies.

That evening, as every evening, he let me in. I was far beyond anger and fury that, even after two years of marriage, his key was still in the back of our front door. I had long since realised that it must be some macho thing, that the woman was being admitted upon the male's sufferance only. What a lot of shit. At that time I never suspected the real reason.

I was allowed to close the door myself while he went back to his computer.

On the floor in the middle of the living room I noticed a ball. A shiny, colorful child's ball, just bigger than a tennis ball. "Been having fun?" I asked.

"What's that, Angel Baby?"

"Been having a little kick about?"

He seemed genuinely puzzled when he turned round. "Sorry?"

I indicated the ball.

"That's nice," he said. "Where did you get it?"

Oh God, here we go, and I was hardly in the front door.

"What do you mean where did I get it? I haven't seen it before."

"Neither have I."

"But it was there on the floor, when I came in."

"You didn't bring it in with you?"

"Like fuck, I did. What's the matter with you? Where did it come from?"

"I dunno. Probably your friend's kid."

"My friend… You talking about Marion? Gary, that was four weeks ago they came to visit."

He shrugged. "Nothing to do with me. Maybe the boy left it and its just rolled out from somewhere."

"Tommy didn't bring a ball - "

"He must have done."

"No, he brought a coloring book and some robot thing. Certainly no ball."

"Well, he obviously did and you can't remember. Why else would it be in the flat?"

"And what? The ball just took it into its head to roll out four weeks later? Have we had an earthquake or something?"

He sighed patiently. "Angel Baby, now you're hallucinating." He turned and recommenced his tap-tapping on the keyboard. "Get rid of the thing, will you?"

42

The doctors thought I could have a problem with one of my kidneys. One of them appeared not to be functioning properly (my kidneys, not the doctors), but they were unsure whether there was just a stone that was too big to pass or something more serious. Could this explain all my illnesses?

Rather than slice me open, they wanted to put a camera in first to see what was there. Just a day job, going in through the groin, sounds worse than it is, a simple twenty minute procedure, local anaesthetic, bring someone with you as you'll feel a bit groggy.

As always, Gary was reluctant, but after the usual verbal sparring (you can write the script yourself by now) he agreed to come. "I'll have to bring my laptop, though. I've got an important review deadline." Okay, whatever. He brought the laptop and a book with him, both encased in neatly-fitting plastic bags with sealed tops – almost as if the things were sterilised.

I had a private room. Blood test done, they came to get me. Gary was sitting in the easy chair a little distance from the bed. It reminded me of the first time I had ever seen him, at Clive's bedside. Only this time he was too busy with his laptop to take any notice of the patient.

"How long are we going to be?" I asked.

"Twenty minutes for the procedure, back up here within the hour," replied the nurse.

"I'll see you in an hour then, Gary," I said as I was wheeled out the door.

"Okay, Angel Baby." No kiss, no touch, preoccupied.

The procedure was extremely painful, despite the doctor saying that I should not have any feeling in my kidney. It was excruciating. The pain was so great, I wanted to pass out. I thought I was going to be sick. I was moaning and I could not keep still.

The damn local in my groin had hardly any affect. I was in such pain that they decided to put me out. I felt a prick in my arm as the sedation went in. And then, mercifully, nothing – at least for what seemed like the briefest of moments. Then I was aware of pain again. I could not open my eyes (had they taped them?) but I heard two women talking. They were concerned. "The blood's very thin. Shit!"

Then I was gone again. Another millisecond in Carly-time, and then I could hear quietness. I tried my eyes. No tape. Slowly I opened them. I was in a small recovery room.

A nurse who I hadn't seen before was standing over me. She wore a surgical gown and hat, but no mask to hide her pretty smile. "Hello, Carly."

"Hi. C – can I have some water?"

"Sure. But just a little now. Sip it." She held my head, and the best water I had ever tasted touched my lips.

"Is it finished?" I asked.

"All over. They had a few problems stopping you bleeding, but they sorted it."

"I seem to remember something. How long have I been out?"

"Four hours."

Had I been able to shoot upright in bed, I would have done. Instead I just groaned. "Four hours! It was only supposed to take twenty minutes!" As I said that, I became aware of the tubes in the back of my hand. What had happened? Had something gone wrong?

"Your blood was much thinner than they realised. Then they couldn't get hold of the physician to come and fix you."

"Was – was I in danger?"

"Of course not! It just took longer than we thought, that's all."

Four hours… "My husband. He must have come looking for me."

The nurse looked puzzled. "No, no one's come looking for you. I didn't know your husband was here. They probably kept him updated downstairs."

An hour later I was back in my room. There was Gary, still sitting there, laptop closed, book open. They made me comfortable on the bed, then he came over and sat beside me. He stroked my forehead. "Welcome back, Angel Baby."

Fucking Angel Baby, how I hated those words. "Where were you?"

"I was here."

"I was supposed to be gone an hour, it's now been nearly five."

"I did try and find somebody, but I couldn't. So I just got on with my work. I knew you were in safe hands."

So safe, I could have bled to death.

The physician came to see me fifteen minutes later, and he explained everything that had happened. And he gave me news that I had not expected to hear: there was nothing wrong with my kidney. They had found nothing untoward in there. Yes, it was good news, but it was also puzzling. They could not find anything wrong with me.

I was not making up my problems. I was not.

No explanation. That was fast becoming the story of my life. Things happening with no explanation as to who, why, how. Just one common denominator: me.

Post op, naturally I felt sore in my stomach and in my groin, but what was really causing me the most discomfort were – my feet. They felt tender and bruised, as if I had run a marathon.

The physician had no explanation for it, but he agreed that there was some discoloration of my soles.

I kept it to myself, but I knew something else was starting: the discoloration of my *soul*.

43

They kept me in hospital for two more days, and then I was allowed home with my discolored soles and soul.

At this time, Gary was working on a freelance basis for a big 5th Avenue advertising agency. It was Christmas, and the company's lavish Christmas party was taking place the following week.

"I really want you to come, Angel Baby. It's very important," importuned the green eyes and their owner.

I was sitting in my dressing gown in the living room, sore and yes, perhaps feeling a little sorry for myself. "Gary, I can't. I just came out of hospital two days ago. I can hardly walk, can hardly go up and down stairs. What could I do at a party? I can't dance right now."

"But it's really important that you're there. It's another three days yet, you'll be fine by then. For me, Angel."

I resisted, he insisted. And of course he won.

He was in the office that day, so I was to join him at the party in the evening. He had told me what he wanted me to wear, right down to my red G-string (with which, of course, he was familiar). He had chosen a sleeveless, knee-length black diamante dress that I had had for a couple of years. I had to admit it was perfect for the occasion – but I would have liked to have some say in the selection myself.

Typical New York in December: it was freezing and pouring down with rain. Soon the snow would come. A warm but rather lengthy taxi journey up town during the tail end of the rush hour kept me dry. You might know the building I went to, a big glass-fronted monolith up by 52nd Street. As the cab pulled up, I could see my husband in amongst the throng of business revellers on the First Floor. His back was towards the entrance and he was talking to a group of three other men.

Quickly I ran from the taxi to the front door, avoiding most of the puddles in the forecourt. A big, black security guard in an immaculate suit, shirt and tie was vetting arrivals. I smiled, expecting to be let in.

"Ma'm?"

"Hi. I'm Gary's wife."

"Do you have an invitation?"

"No. Gary, in there. My husband."

"Gary who?" A palm pilot had appeared in his hand.

"Goffrey. Gary Goffrey. Without a D."

He tapped on the machine. He shook his head. "I have no one by that name on the staff list."

"No, he's a freelance. Gary. He's there, right there. The tall one in the black shirt with his back to us."

The doorman looked around. "Please wait here, ma'm."

Oh for God's sake. I was standing there, five days out of hospital, shivering to death with just a pashmina around my shoulders, and I had Johnny Jobsworth to contend with. "Please hurry up."

The security guard went inside and discreetly sidled up to Gary and spoke into his ear. Gary said something, making the guard repeat what he said, and then Gary turned, looked at me, paused to think and then followed the guard back to the front door. The guard opened the door and then stayed behind at a tactful distance. Gary came out, glass of red wine in his hand. "Hi, Angel Baby. What are you doing here?"

At that moment I could have killed him. I had fallen for it

again.

"Like, I've come for the party? Duh?" I didn't care if he or the guard heard the sarcasm in my voice. If they wanted to cut it with a knife they could have done, but I would have preferred the knife to be in Gary's back.

"Oh yeh," Gary sipped his wine. "I forgot to tell you. You're not invited. Sorry."

"What do you mean, I'm not invited?"

"Staff only. No partners. They told me this afternoon."

"So why the fuck didn't you phone me to tell me?"

"Sorry. I forgot. Busy and all that."

"So, I'm just going to have to go back, am I?"

"Well, yeh, obviously."

Without further word, I turned and walked away into the rain.

A graze on your knee

Georgie sat hugging his knees in the corner of the cellar. He was smiling to himself.

Daddy was bad, wasn't he? Very, very bad. And that meant he was good.

And that meant Georgie was pleased, because when Daddy was pleased, he was too.

Daddy was allowing him out now, more frequently. He had nearly gotten caught when he left his ball out. There had been no formal introduction. Mommy had seen him but she had not realised.

Good. That meant he could play with Mommy some more.

Georgie liked this new house. His cellar was cosy. The one problem was that it had nothing on the floor, no carpets or rugs. So when Georgie was kneeling down doing what he did – doing what he was told to do – his knees would get sore.

The last time they had kept him there for so long that his right knee was actually grazed and bleeding at the end of the session.

Now he sat with his knees tucked under his chin. He could smell the graze. He could smell his blood.

Softly, his tongue came out and he started licking his wound. A small piece of skin touched his teeth. He bit it off and began to chew it...

Is it time to start the hard core stuff, Daddy?

PART FOUR

The man of my dreams

44

My sleep had not been good for a long time. Or perhaps it had been too good. Our sex life was diminishing rapidly, so my evenings consisted of inane chatter, perhaps one of his little mind games, dinner, a glass of wine (white only nowadays) or a cup of tea, then off to bed on my own, leaving my husband on his computer. I would fall asleep as soon as my head touched the pillow.

I didn't have any more twenty-one hour sleep marathons, but when I awoke each morning I would feel exhausted – as if my ka had been out of my body all night on adventures of its own.

Which it might well have done…

That night, I had been asleep for about three hours when suddenly I was awake again. For a moment I was bewildered. What had happened? I had felt something pricking the bottom of my leg. Was there a pin in the bed? Was there a mosquito? It was summertime in sweltering, swampy New York and I was prone to the bastards.

I shook my head. This was unusual to be awake at this time. Did I want to pee? Normally I could last all night (oh to be able to do that nowadays!). I didn't feel any pressure, but seeing as I was awake I might as well have one.

I was aware that Gary was not in bed next to me. Was he still on the damn computer? He should have married the bloody thing instead of me. Mr Gary and Mrs Vaio Goffrey – still without a D.

I threw back the bedclothes and nearly fell as I stood up. The floor seemed further away than usual – which meant that the bed seemed higher than usual. How strange.

My co-ordination must have been off, because I missed the bedroom door by a few feet. I found it, five feet further to the right than I had calculated, and then I thought *Why don't you put the light on, you silly bitch?*

As my right hand opened the door, my left hand flicked on the light switch.

Looking out into the corridor, I froze.

What the hell…?

This was not my apartment.

I was in an upstairs corridor of an old manor house. The light from my open bedroom door illuminated thick red carpet and dark wooden-clad walls with portraits hung at precise intervals all the way along. *What?* Where the hell was I?

"Gary?" I called. "Gary?"

The place was deathly quiet. "Gary?"

The light from behind me began to move sideways and reduce as my bedroom door swung shut. Quickly I stuck out my hand to stop it closing all the way. It was an irrational reaction as I knew we had no locks on the door.

But this was not *my* bedroom, was it?

Gingerly I took my hand away. The door stayed where it was.

As I was wondering whether to forgo the pee and run back into bed and cover myself up, I heard a noise. It sounded like a groan, a dull, intense groan, coming from somewhere to my right. "Gary?" I whispered.

My bare feet made no sound on the luxurious carpet. Only as I looked down at them did I realise that, of course, it was not only my feet that were bare. I always slept in the nude. I was stark naked, walking along a corridor in a strange old house in the middle of the night.

I didn't, as you might expect, look at the pictures on the wall as I went past. I wasn't going to add to my spookiness.

The next door was about ten feet along. I stood outside it and listened. The noise was coming from inside.

Telling myself I shouldn't be doing this, I reached out and turned the handle. The door swung open noiselessly.

It was another bedroom.

I stood and stared.

Inside, Gary was kneeling on the floor. He was naked and his hands were tied behind his back with black plastic rope. His feet were also tied. There was a transparent tube going into his left nostril, the kind of tube I was attached to in hospital. It was about a yard long. At the other end of the tube and standing naked in front of Gary, was a famous gay actor. His dick was stuck into a siphon in the top of the tube and he was ejaculating down it furiously and continuously.

There was a terrified look on Gary's face as he looked towards me.

But, terrified or not, Gary had an erection that would have put Priapus to shame…

With a jolt I was back in bed. And I was awake again. I was sweating. Propping myself up on my elbows, I was in the process of thanking God that it had been just a dream when my breath caught on the exhale.

This was still not my apartment. It was modern and brighter, but it was still not my place.

Okay, I'll go with this. Was I to get up again? There was no indication, but obviously I was here for some reason, so I obliged.

The bedroom door was in the same place as it had been in the manor house. Outside, the corridor was much shorter and there was a door directly opposite mine. There was a light shining from inside and those same muffled sounds from within.

Should I do what was expected of me? Like hell was I going to, I wasn't going to play this game. I turned back – but my bedroom door had disappeared. I was faced with just corridor wall. I looked to the left then to the right. The only door in the whole corridor was now the one which was currently behind me.

Clever. Okay, I'll do this if it's what you want. Then can I go back to sleep?

Without stealth or pretence, I opened the door. All my senses were assailed.

My hearing was assailed by Cher's Greatest Hits playing from a dockable iPod on my left.

My smell was assailed by the unmistakable aroma of marijuana.

My taste was assailed by the fug of smoke, sweat and bleach that was in the room.

My vision was assailed by the sight of Gary, bare on the floor with two other naked men, one with his cock in Gary's mouth, the other with his cock rammed so far into Gary's ass that they looked like conjoined twins.

But, worst of all, my touch was assailed by something wet, slippery and sticky. I looked down and saw that I was assaulting myself with my right hand. Savagely, viciously, I was pulling at my own sex, my juices running along my arm and dripping onto the floor like blood from an open wound...

I felt the weight on my belly milliseconds before I felt his hands around my throat. The hands were smooth and delicate, and yet they applied a surprising force against my windpipe as I lay on the bed. My husband had flipped. This was the real Gary and he was trying to murder me.

Keeping my eyes closed, I groaned and forced myself to smile, make him think I thought he was having sex with me. I tried to say something, but the pressure on my throat was so strong no sound would come out. But still I smiled. If this is going to be it, you bastard, I'm not going to let you see I'm scared. I'll die grinning. You won't like that, will you?

Only with the grin was I aware of something in my mouth. Something soft yet firm. My teeth were together, so he must have pushed it in there before he started to kill me.

I moved my tongue, simultaneously aware of two other things.

Gary was between my legs now and was fucking me.

And the thing in my mouth was a piece of orange.

45

This time Gary was next to me when I woke up, and I was back in my own apartment. His breathing was regular and I thought he was asleep, but as I got out of bed he said, "Hi."

I was still a little bewildered and confused. That wasn't the first night I had had bad dreams, and I suspected it wouldn't be the last. But I was relieved that I was back to reality – as perverse and uncomfortable as reality was.

"Hi," I responded.

"Did you sleep well, my Angel Baby?" Gary stretched, the sheet falling down to expose his hairy chest.

"No, I didn't. I... I'm going to have my shower."

"Did you have those dreams again?"

"Uh-huh."

"Do you want to tell me all about them?"

I shook my head. "No, I don't..." Then I changed my mind. "Yes, I think I do." I sat back down on the bed. "I was in this mansion..."

He listened intently as I told him two of the three things that had happened last night. I didn't say anything about him strangling me. "Wow," he said at the end. "Anything else?"

"No, nothing. That's enough, isn't it? You're in my dreams, these things are happening to you, and I'm watching them happen."

"That must be awful, my Angel Baby. But they're just dreams."

I stood up off the bed. "Like shit they are, they're bloody nightmares." I walked off for my shower, wondering if Gary had noticed that I had observed his erection underneath the sheets.

The slightly too hot water cascaded over my body. It was wonderful. Soon, I knew, I would have to look down or study myself in the mirror and see what had appeared overnight this time, but just for a minute or two I pushed these things out of my mind.

There were no bruises around my neck, as one might have expected, but there were distinct finger-sized bruises on my inner thighs. Had he done that to me? Or had I done it to myself when I was watching?

And there was a small scab on the bottom of my right leg. It wasn't a mosquito bite.

Back in the bedroom, there was a used tissue on Gary's bedside table. He was still lying there and seemed genuinely asleep. Post coital, I guessed – even if the coitus was with his right hand.

"Gary? Gary!" I was standing at the end of the bed. Sleepy eyes opened and looked at me, as always with that same loving, condescending smile.

"Look at me." I pointed down below.

The smile turned into a grin. "Very nice. But don't you have to go to work?"

"Not my pussy, look at my thighs!" I opened my legs slightly. "Look at the bruises."

"How did you get those?"

"How should I know? Do you have any ideas?"

He shrugged. "You've not been well, have you Angel Baby? You probably just keep walking into tables or something, you know your balance isn't good."

"What do you mean 'walking into tables'? The bruises aren't even in the right place!"

"Well, I don't know. They're your bruises."

"And look at my arms." I had noticed light but distinct scratches on both my forearms.

"Look at your *wrists*," he countered. Now he was not hiding the condescension.

"What?"

"Your jewellery. Perhaps you should take your bracelets off before you go to bed?" He turned, his indication that the conversation was over.

46

That was not the only time I had bad 'dreams' or woke up with marks on my body. A few times I woke up with little cuts on the side of my mouth, the little tears you often get after a visit to the dentist. They would be accompanied by a pain in my skull, as if I had bumped my head or something had hit it. I could feel no blood, no scab, but my head was really sore.

I asked Gary to have a look at my head, but he said he couldn't see anything. I didn't believe him, and sure enough when I looked in the mirror I could see a two inch red mark under my hair. Gary still said he couldn't see it, but he couldn't deny the little cuts on my mouth.

But, as always, he had a reasonable explanation for it. My bracelets again. Naturally I would move my arms in my sleep – especially if I was having those dreams that I had to recount to him in explicit detail – and maybe I had touched my mouth, maybe I had even sucked on my bracelets.

From that day, I never wore any jewellery to bed again.

And, surprise, surprise, the cuts on the mouth stopped.

47

By now, two and a half years into my marriage, I had gone off Gary sexually. I considered him a creep and a pervert. Things were happening to me which had never happened to me before in my life until he came along. Was he doing it? Always there were the reasonable explanations, but I had no doubt he was behind things.

Either that or I was going mad.

I couldn't get wet for him, but he still forced himself on me. I let him do it in the hope that sex now might mollify the 'punishment' of the bad dreams afterwards. It seemed to work. No sex, bad dreams. Sex, no dreams.

But it was so painful. At first I tried not to cry out when he was chafing me. I did once, and it only heightened his pleasure and he came inside me immediately and ferociously. I didn't want to give him pleasure, but my gasping, my submissiveness was obviously a turn-on for him. The more painful it appeared for me, the quicker he would be finished. So I became a screamer. Sad thing was, I wasn't acting.

I went to see the nurse at my local surgery. She thought maybe I had an infection. She hardly needed to examine me to agree that I looked sore down there, and a bit swollen. She took a swab, but there was no tell-tale mucus or pee (or come). It seemed there was no infection, just an over-energetic use of my sex.

Over-energetic? Two times a week for five minutes?

I was told to carry on enjoying myself and let a tube of *KY Jelly* become my new best friend.

Treat me as a whore

Georgie had no time to sit hugging his knees tonight. Daddy had told him tonight was going to be one of those nights.

So Georgie had washed carefully, every crevice of his body. Daddy liked cleanliness.

Now he was just waiting for Daddy to appear.

Tonight he was to be allowed upstairs.

To play.

48

I awoke with a start. The bedside clock said 04:00.

There had been a light. A bright orange flash of light had gone off in my face. Had the dream of a flashing light awoken me, or had I been waking up and been aware of a light in the room?

"What the hell was that?" I lay on my back with my eyes open, adjusting from the flash and to the dark.

"What was what?" So Gary was awake beside me.

"Did you just flash a torch in my face or something?"

"No. Of course not."

I raised myself onto my elbows. I had kicked the bedsheet off me in my sleep and I was lying there naked. "Did you just turn the light on quickly, on and off?"

"No. Why should I do that?"

"I… I don't know. That's really strange. Something just woke me up."

"Another one of your dreams?"

My heart was thumping a little. God, this was ridiculous. "I don't know."

"Get back to sleep, Angel Baby."

"I need a pee."

"No, no," he reached out and put his hand on my arm. "Get back to sleep quickly or you'll never get off again."

"Gary," I moved my arm away. "I want to pee – and no, don't even think about it. I'm going to the john."

I was aware of his eyes on my butt as I walked across the room in the darkness. Then I stopped suddenly in the open doorway. "Did you hear that?"

"Hear what?"

"I'm sure I heard something. A sound. In the living room."

"I can hear nothing, Angel Baby."

"Not now, it's stopped. Just now."

In the half light, he was sitting up in bed. "It's another of your dreams, Carly. It's just you. A nightmare. Come back to bed."

Maybe he was right, of course and as always, but I was sure it wasn't a dream. I had been woken up by a flashing light. I'll agree that the sound in the living room may or may not have been real. Perhaps I was just spooked.

"Come on," said the mellifluous voice. "Don't go out there if you're scared. We have another way of getting rid of your pee, don't we? We haven't done it for a long, long time."

He put his head back down on the pillows, smiling, waiting for me.

I was up early the next morning. The pillowcases would need changing. I would pop them in the washing machine before I went to work and allow the pillows to air for the day.

In the living room, the balcony door was open. Not wide and gaping, as if an intruder had been disturbed and had fled, it was just open. And that never happened. Gary was a stickler for security. At night, the windows and balcony door out the front would be closed. During the day, if he was in, a window would be open just a few inches for air; if he was out, it would be closed.

There was no way Gary – who was always the last to come to bed, me having collapsed exhausted way earlier – would have left the balcony door open.

So what did that mean? Had someone been in?

I looked around the room. Nothing had been disturbed, nothing seemed to be missing. I was about to call to Gary when I thought better of it. I had a better idea. I would leave the balcony door exactly as it was – and I wouldn't say a word. See if he said anything.

I could hear him moving in the bedroom. It was the same sort of sound that I had heard coming from the living room last night. Then I thought of something, and I hurried out to the front door.

The door was locked but the security chain was not connected. And that was something else that never happened. The chain was always on at night.

Had Gary had somebody here last night? Had the balcony door been open to air any tell-tale human scent from the living room?

Gary had been awake already when I woke. Had my waking and what we did afterwards stopped him from going out to tidy up? To chain the front door and close the balcony window?

And what about the flashing light? My husband was a photographer and he moved in that world. Surely what I was thinking couldn't be right. I had been lying there naked on the bed with the sheets pulled back...

Gary never did mention the open balcony door.

49

I have mentioned before how I was notorious amongst my friends for the explosive capability of my rectum. I don't care what you girls say, I am on the boys' side in this: there is nothing – absolutely nothing – to beat the sheer pleasure of a rip-roaring, stomach extending, room-clearing fart.

One morning I got out of bed and thought maybe I had been a little over-keen during the sheet-trembler I had done five minutes ago. I could feel something small but distinct poking out of my butt. I thought it was a turtle head (one in the departure lounge, you know what I mean). Cheeks clenched, I went into the bathroom.

I sat down and wiped myself. *Christ, that hurt.* And there was no poo on the paper but slight traces of blood.

Tentatively, carefully, I put my index finger up my butt. I couldn't believe what I felt. Oh my God, this I wanted to see.

Had Gary come into the bathroom at that moment he would have thought all his Christmases had come at once. There I was, back to the mirror, bending over from the waist, legs open, pulling my butt cheeks wide apart and trying to see up my own asshole.

The cause of my discomfort was clear: I had a bunch of grapes hanging from my bottom. Pinot noir, probably (I had consumed enough of it over the years).

Shit – figuratively. Literally it would have been just too painful. I thought of poor Clive and now knew what he must have gone through. But at least he had been using his a-hole for something additional to waste disposal. I hadn't.

Had I?

When I told him, Gary was fascinated, and he wanted to prod and poke, but I clenched my cheeks back together quickly (painful and, much to his pleasure, I caught his finger in there) and, once again, I set off to see the nurse.

She said my piles were classic signs of constipation (well actually, if anything I was the opposite of constipated, but I didn't argue). Surgery was an option in the future, but first 'we' would try a course of cream and pessaries.

So that was my life for a while. I'd go off to do a job for the day, maybe meet a friend for lunch, carry about a bunch of pinot noirs up my butt (and wonder how the hell I really got them), go home to my husband, not get in without him opening the door, *would you like a drink Angel Baby?*, have something to eat, go for an exhausted sleep, and either have the real nightmare of Gary having so-sore sex with me or the query unreal nightmare of Gary having sex with other men. Still sometimes I would wake up with bruises, but there were no more cut mouths or scratches.

Great, huh?

PART FIVE

The end approaches

50

On the few occasions I would get back from work and Gary would be out, I would be relieved. As I mentioned, I could tell whether he was out if the window was open or not.

On those occasions, I would leave *my* key in the door. So it was his turn not to be able to get in. Knock on *my* door, buddy.

Regularly, I would go through his drawers. One day I noticed he had cut all the labels out of his clothes. Strange, but I suppose some people do that. But why all of a sudden, after three years of marriage? All his clothes were black except for one grey V-neck jumper I had bought him in Macy's. He would only wear it inside the house, never outside. Outside, it was always black.

Then shortly after this, I found that the labels had been cut out of some of my clothes too. I challenged him on this and, as always, this very sweet and reasonable man had an answer: for some reason, recently his labels had begun to scratch and irritate him. He thought it might be the detergent. To save his Angel Baby from the discomfort he had experienced, he had started to cut the labels out of her clothes too.

"Well, thanks very much Gary," I said tight-lipped across the kitchen table. "But if I want the labels cut out of my clothes, I'll do it."

"Okay, Angel Baby."

∞

Again I noticed that some of my clothes were being washed when I hadn't worn them. It was now spring, so he couldn't say it had been cold.

The day after I had found the latest batch, I forced myself to be sprightly when I came home. Much to his surprise, I gave him a wifely hug – and noticed his jumper was moving up and down on something silky. One of my camisoles perhaps?

I 'accidentally' lifted his jumper up as I pulled out of the clinch (dammit, he still smelt so bloody good), and sure enough there was my red cami underneath.

"Gary! What's this?"

"Fancy a cup of tea, love?" He went towards the kitchen.

"You're wearing my clothes again."

"Sorry? What? Oh, this? Carly, you know how I can't stand wool next to my skin. This jumper you gave me is very woolly, it irritates me. I want to wear it because you gave it to me, but I won't be able to unless I have something underneath. I chose something smooth and silky. It feels nice. And now I can wear my Angel Baby's present!"

51

One day when I was cleaning the living room, I noticed something thin and shiny on the floor. I stopped the Dyson before it could suck it up and bent forward to pick up the object. Just in time I realised what it was and I pulled my hand back.

"Gary!"

He strolled in from the kitchen, eating his breakfast bagel (salami and cheese). He smiled.

"What's this?" I pointed to the object on the floor.

The smile did not waver, but he frowned in curiosity. He came over and bent down. Then he realised what it was and picked it up, showing it to me.

"It's a hypodermic needle, isn't it?" I said.

"Yep. There's more in the drawer." He pulled open the bottom drawer of his computer desk and pointed to half a dozen of the things sealed in packages.

"Where the hell did you get those from?"

He looked sheepish. "Well, actually, when you were at the hospital again the other day and the nurse went out of the room? They were just lying there on her trolley?"

"Gary!"

"I know, I know. But they're much better for the ink on the printer cartridges than the plastic syringes they give you. St

Vincent's won't miss a few. God knows your insurance has paid for them over the years."

Always, always, always, the reasonable excuse.
  Always.
  It was driving me mad.

52

We were still having sex. Irregularly now, brief and very painful, and yet I still came sometimes (well, a girl has needs as well). My pussy was still sore and swollen but, of course, my pain seemed to excite him. There was always copious amounts of semen flowing from me the following morning. He came like three or four men.

During one of our five minute shags, I noticed that he was pricking my chest more than usual.

A look at my sleeping husband the next morning confirmed what I had suspected: he had begun to shave the hairs on his chest.

It was stupid of me to mention it, because sure enough the Reasonable Excuse was ready. Yes, he was shaving his chest. His hairs were getting coarser as he got older, they were itching him, especially when it got hot in the summer. It was much more comfortable without them.

"But it pricks *me*," I explained. "And anyway, I like men with hair on their chest. It's manly."

Always the considerate one, my manly husband stopped shaving his chest. And went on to *Veet* cream instead.

Less than impressed, I was.

53

It was his birthday. I wanted to do the wifely thing and take him out somewhere for dinner. Actually, no. I didn't *want* to take him out for dinner, but it's the thing wives are expected to do. Thankfully, he saved me the chore.

"Oh, do we have to, Angel Baby?" he said when I mentioned it. "I am so, so busy with the web site. Can't you just cook us something here? I know, let's have a couple of good bottles of wine. Maybe then afterwards we can go make babies!"

Thoughts of our painful sex life made me cringe. I repressed my verbal retaliation until we were eating.

"Obviously you're very aware, Gary," I said as he popped a forkful of rice into his mouth, "that we'll never have children together." We were tucking in to a chicken korma and aloo sag that I had cooked (with help from a Wal-Mart Indian Meal For Two bag).

"No, that's where you're wrong," he waved his fork to make his point. "We're going to have two."

"No we're not. Not at all, I can assure you. I'm never having children with you."

"Well, you're a bit late because I've already decided."

I looked at the nearly empty bottle of wine on the table. Was it that that was talking? Or the four empty *Tiger* beer bottles?

I thought I would humor him. "You've decided? I see. And I get no say in the matter."

"No." His face was open and pleasant. "None at all."

"Okay..."

As if explaining, he said "When you go to sleep, Carly, I don't."

I wondered what was coming this time. "Yes you do, I hear you snoring." I broke a piece of naan bread and mopped up some sauce.

"No, no, that's just my body. When you're asleep, I go there."

Maybe it was me that was drunk. "Go where?"

"Carly, Carly, Carly. Surely you're not that stupid?"

Did I want to get into this? "Obviously I am. Tell me."

"I go to reality."

"I see... Is that the new shop on 32nd Street?"

The green eyes were wide. "Do you think you're living reality, Carly?"

No, I'm living a fucking nightmare. "I know I am. Look a real piece of naan bread. And I can make it disappear!" I popped it into my mouth.

"No, what you're living is a proportion of reality."

"A proportion of reality?"

"Yes."

"All right then. When you go there, where exactly is there?"

He scoffed. "There! I've told you."

"Okay... So what do you do when you actually get *there*?"

"I teach the future."

"You teach the future." I wiped my mouth on a piece of kitchen towel. Caution was telling me to get up and leave now, but curiosity was telling me to wait and see where this was going.

"Actually, I chose you, did you know that?"

"Did you? You chose me." I screwed up the kitchen towel and threw it onto my empty plate. "You know, Gary, I haven't got a clue what you're talking about. You're obviously on another planet. We're not going to have kids, end of story. And I think we should leave the second bottle of wine to another night, don't you?"

He ran his finger across the table top, making small wavy motions. "You won't know because I'll just do it anyway."

"Do what? Have sex with me?"

"Impregnate you. And you'll never know. Admit it, Carly, you like having sex with me."

I said nothing.

"You like having sex with me so much, you'll probably have sex with my dead body."

"Whatever."

"And you know what?" The green eyes looked up and bore into my soul. "I'll have sex with your dead body too."

54

There was a party on at MAC to celebrate the fifth anniversary of their Christopher Street shop. Everyone was there, not only the MAC staff and management (big boss Frank had even flown in from Canada) but some local celebs as well (yes, including Bobby de Niro).

I was out later than usual, but the party was still in full swing when I left just before midnight.

Gary was, of course, waiting up for me, so even at that hour I couldn't get in without him opening the door. We had a glass of wine, white for me and red for him, and I went to bed at 02:00.

At 04:00 I heard that familiar screaming again. My stomach felt like it was turning itself inside out, and I had woken myself up shouting in agony. My body was saturated with sweat. Of all the stomach pains, this was the worst ever.

Gary was awake beside me (had he been asleep?), and he considerately (but very slowly) went into the bathroom and came back with two tylenol. "Take these, Angel Baby, they'll help."

They didn't. By 08:00 I was on my hands and knees crawling around the living room, moaning in agony, shouting in pain, and farting for America. I could not keep still. Moving seemed to help, even if it was on all fours.

My ever-concerned husband had gone back to sleep after he had given me the cure-all tablets and then woke back up to suggest that I go into the living room if I was going to keep shouting all night. "No point in us both losing sleep. I have an important article to write tomorrow."

He hid his surprise well when he came into the living room that morning and saw me on the floor. For a moment I thought he was simply going to step over me, but he stopped and looked down.

"Gary," I looked up at him, "you're going to have to call the paramedics."

He bent forward and the bastard actually stroked my hair. "No, you don't need the paramedics."

"I do."

"Are you going to die? The paramedics are very stretched attending to sick people."

"I'm just ill. I need a hospital."

"No, you'll be fine, Angel Baby. I'll get you some more pills."

"I DON'T NEED SOME MORE PILLS, I NEED THE FUCKING PARAMEDICS!"

"Okay, okay." He held up his hands in placation.

It took twenty minutes for them to arrive. They hardly needed to examine me, there was just this mess in a T-shirt and pants rolling about on the floor, moaning and groaning. While one of the paramedics went to get the stretcher, the other said to Gary, "Can you organise some of her clothes to bring with you?"

"What?" He was aghast. "You want me to come with you?"

"You are her husband, aren't you?"

"Yes, but I've got this important article - "

"Gary!" I growled from floor level.

With a huge sigh, the most put-upon husband in the world made the supreme sacrifice and went to pack a bag for me.

∞

Pain blurs. We got to the hospital. I remember having an X-ray, before which they injected a dye into my arm which they said would burn but I felt nothing. Back in the cubicle in ER, they gave me another, different injection.

We were alone. Gary sat on a wooden chair reading a book he had thoughtfully brought along for himself (in a plastic cover), apparently too engrossed to talk to his wife. I just lay there.

Ten minutes later, the injected drug kicked in and the pain began to fade. The relief was one of the most beautiful feelings I have ever had in my life. If you've been in that position, you'll know what I mean. The pain that had been killing me for six hours had been vanquished. The Death Notices were premature.

A nurse checked in on me a couple of times, and then about an hour later a doctor came in. I think she was the one that had seen me on my arrival, but as all that I had been interested in at the time was dying, I couldn't be sure.

"Well, Mrs Godfrey, you look a lot better than when you came in. Has the injection helped?"

"Yes, thank you. I can't tell you how better I feel."

The doctor turned to Gary. "Mr Godfrey, can you tell me what happened with your wife this morning."

Nothing. Gary continued reading his book.

"Mr Godfrey?"

"Gary," I tried to reach out and knock the book, but he was too far away. "The doctor's talking to you."

He looked up, his eyes dreamy. "Mm?" It was as if the doctor was not there.

"I know exactly what it is, doctor," I said. "I've got food poisoning."

The doctor turned her back to Gary. "Have you now?"

"Yes, I went out last night and I was being a bit of a pig."

"Well, I think I'll be the judge of whether you've got food poisoning or not. Have you been sick? Diarrhoea?"

"No. Severe gas, though." On precise cue, my butt emitted a silent pop. They would know about it in a minute.

"I don't think it's food poisoning," said the doctor. "I thought maybe it could be a kidney stone – the pain, the inability to keep still. Classic symptoms. But nothing showed up on the X-ray. You may have passed it. But at least you're not in pain now."

"No. I actually feel quite good. Drained, though."

"Yes, you would after what you've been through. Rest here for a few minutes, then you can go."

As the doctor was stepping through the curtains, Gary said, "It's Goffrey."

The doctor stopped. "I'm sorry?"

His green eyes were as hard and emotionless as marble. "Not Godfrey. She's not Mrs Godfrey. It's Goffrey. Without a D."

"Oh… Right."

"Wouldn't want my wife to be confused with someone else now, would we?" He smiled the coldest, unmeant smile I had ever seen and then went back to his book.

The doctor left without another word – just as my fart hit Gary and he sniffed in disgust.

55

Sometimes I would ask my friends around for the evening. By now they all knew about Gary and his Little Ways. Despite that, not one of my friends ever baulked at the idea of spending an evening at my place. Bless them, because the less I was on my own with him, the better.

One evening, Jacqui and Tracy came round to watch a video. I considered it only fair that I warn Gary beforehand. I asked him not to talk to them about his boring computer stuff because they were not interested. To them, and to me, a megabyte was what we took out of one of Starbuck's paninis. Gary had done it before; he would know my friends did not know what he was talking about and he would talk technical on purpose to make them feel stupid.

Sure enough, Jacqui came into the living room and Tracy was hardly through the front door, when he said "Jacqui, pop over here and look at what I've done on the computer. I think you'll like this."

"She won't, Gary," I snapped while my friend looked embarrassed.

"But I think Jac might be interested."

"She isn't."

He just shrugged and grinned.

I had used the VCR the evening before to try out the movie I had bought (a Bargain Bucket umpteenth-release edition of *Basic Instinct*). Last night the machine had worked fine. Tonight us three girls sat there with our wine and chips – and the damn machine wouldn't even take the tape, let alone play it.

We must have fiddled with it for half an hour, plugging and unplugging it, pressing every conceivable combination of buttons, even using force. But the machine would not swallow the tape. It was dead, no lights, nothing.

It was Gary's VCR, one of the things he had brought from Australia, so it had one of those strange three-pin plugs on it with an adaptor for our two-pin sockets.

"Maybe the amp's buggered in the plug or something?" suggested my English friend Tracy.

From across the room came the comment, "Fuse, darling, fuse. Amps don't get buggered, you don't buy them in a shop." His *faux*-English accent was insulting.

We ignored him. I said to Tracy, "I was watching it last night," I looked across at Gary. "The *amp's* fine."

"No harm in looking," said my practical friend. "Got a screwdriver?"

I got one from the kitchen drawer. "I hope it's not the *amp*," I said as I handed it to her. "We haven't got any spare ones." Gary pretended not to hear.

It didn't take Tracy a second to have the back off the plug. "Da-dah!" She held up the plug to show us.

The wires were connected but the fuse was missing. It had been taken out.

The three of us looked across at Gary. Blithely, calmly, he was continuing with his work. After a moment he said, "I told you it wasn't the amp."

56

More and more now I was spending evenings with my friends, either in my apartment (with the ever-present Gary) or out in a bar or around one of their places. I just did not want to be alone with my husband more than I had to be.

Was there a precise moment when I stopped loving him? Did I ever stop loving him? Let me expand on that: do we ever stop loving someone, completely and fully? Once this strange emotion has entered our soul, do we ever get rid of it? We might call it something different, that's why we say there is a fine line between love and hate – when in fact there should be a gap the size of the universe. Does love really turn to hate at all, or is hate just a word for a different form of love?

Does this explain why couples stay together long after the relationship sell-by date has passed? Because, whatever the abuser does to the abusee, they still love each other?

I have never had any truck with these poor bitches who get beaten half to death and then immediately go back to the bastard ("But I love him!"), only to come ever closer to death within days. But my theory might explain their stupidity.

Or is it something more insidious? Humans are a species prone to addiction: do we become addicted to the abuse? Like drugs that we know we should not take, that we know will surely kill us in the end, do we stay for more abuse because we are addicted to it?

Was I addicted to it? Or was it that I had fallen in love with Gary and, according to Carly's Theory, once in love always in love?

One evening, I made one of my irregular phone calls to my Dad. At that time, he was living in Geneva, Switzerland. I didn't quite know what to say, not least because the ubiquitous Gary was there in the apartment, but my Dad seemed to know something was wrong even before I said anything.

"Is everything all right between you two, Carly?" he asked.

"Dad, it… Well, life's hard, you know." He would know I couldn't speak freely.

"I know, darling."

"You do?"

"More than you think. There's no need to say anything. Know that I'm always thinking about you. Tell you what, you're going to Arizona soon, aren't you?"

I had job on a movie being shot down in Tucson Studios.

"Day after tomorrow."

"Well, why don't you get that son-in-law of mine to give me a call while you're away?"

"Okay. Actually, he's here now if you want to have a chat."

"No, no, another time. I'll talk to him while you're away. You have a good time in Arizona, now. And remember, I'm only a phone call away."

"Thanks, Dad." How could a thirty second phone call make me feel so much better?

"My Dad has asked you to call him," I said after I had hung up. "Says you two haven't had a chat for ages."

"Mm," said Gary without looking up from the screen.

Arizona was good. The movie looked like it was going to be good (the remake of *3:10 To Yuma* was to be a resounding success), and the people were good. In fact, one of the stunt co-ordinators on the project showed a lot of interest in me – interest which was more than reciprocated. But no, I was not naughty. During my marriage, I remained physically faithful.

I had no contact from Gary for the whole seven days I was away, which was mighty strange for the man who would ring me if I was one minute late home at night. But it was also refreshing. What was I complaining about?

On my return home, Gary was pleased to see me (I was so glad that wasn't a gun in his pocket), and after my experiences in Arizona I was in need of a little relief myself.

Afterwards, as we lay there, Gary said, "I tried to phone your Dad."

"You did?"

"Several times. He was always out. But I eventually got him last night. Sends his love."

"What did he want to talk to you about?"

"Oh, he just wanted to say 'Hi' to his son-in-law. He's a good man, your Dad. Said he'll ring you."

It was a couple of nights later. I had spent an hour or so with Jacqui and Tracy in Julius' Restaurant, near MAC in Christopher Street. As Gary let me in he told me that my Dad had just called. "You just missed him, out with your friends again."

"Shit, I'll ring him back." I dashed over to the phone.

"No, no," Gary held up his hand. "He says not to. He's going out. He'll give you a call next week sometime."

The call from Dad never came, but that wasn't unusual. Dad was like that. Typical man, if he had something to say, he would ring. If he hadn't, he wouldn't.

Then, four weeks later, he phoned – and I was out again. Gary told me Dad said he would ring earlier tomorrow night. But still I missed him, even though I came straight home from work. Once again, Dad was going out. He would try me again the next day.

Am I naïve? Does it take me a long time to cotton on? I had to allow for the time difference between us and Europe, so after the shop closed the next evening I rang him at home directly from the office. He was pleased to hear from me. He thought I would have called him sooner.

"But you've just kept missing me! Each time you've phoned."

"Literally, I miss you, darling. But I haven't phoned you."

"I'm sorry?"

"I haven't phoned you."

"What, not at all?"

"Not since we spoke before you went to Arizona."

"But when you spoke to Gary, you said you would ring me when I got back."

"I haven't spoken to Gary."

"What do you mean? He rang you when I was away, like you asked."

"No, he didn't. And frankly I didn't expect him to. The last time I spoke to Gary was three years ago at your wedding."

I could have cried. I *was* crying. "What?" I said softly.

"Carly, there's something you should know. It's why I asked you to ask him to ring me while you were away. Five weeks ago, Gary sent me a fax."

"A fax?" From Mr Computer, Mr E-mail?

"Yes."

"What did it say?"

"It's how I knew you were unhappy. He said you were constantly being ill. That you were hallucinating, imagining things. Always accusing him of the most bizarre behaviour. That you were spending money you hadn't got and had to dip into your inheritance. That you were heavily in debt. He said he wanted to get you help but couldn't afford it…"

Oh my God.

"How much did he ask for?"

"Twenty thousand dollars."

"What! Dad, tell me you never - "

"Oh no, no. I think I know my own daughter better than that. That's why I wanted to talk to him."

"And why he didn't want to talk to you."

"Quite."

"What are you going to do, Dad?"

"Nothing. Do *you* want some money, darling?"

"No, Dad, no. I'm not in debt. I haven't even touched Grandma's inheritance. Whatever you do, don't send me any money."

"So the question is, what are *you* going to do, Carly?"

I thought, then I said "Something I should have done a long time ago."

57

That was it. It was over. Marriage was not for life, who was I kidding? I had been a fool from the outset. 'Falling in love with love.' I had stuck with this man for over three years. I had put up with his weirdness, his little mind games, his rudeness to others, his brutal sex, kidding myself that it was 'just his way'. I had even pretended that the marks on my body were not caused by him and whatever he was doing to me while I was asleep.

He had convinced me that I was imagining everything.

But I wasn't imagining the attempt to extort money from my father.

I rehearsed my diatribe on the short walk home from Christopher Street. By the time I reached West 4th I was word perfect.

Then when I reached the house, I stopped in my tracks, staring up at the windows of our apartment. They were closed. Which meant that Gary was out.

You could count on the fingers of one hand the number of times during the marriage that Gary had been out when I came home from work. With a timing which was shocking in its perversity, today had to be one of those days. I felt my vitriol leaking from me like air from a punctured tyre.

Upstairs, I could let myself in. I didn't know whether to laugh or cry. I had decided my marriage was over, and suddenly I could let myself into my own apartment! I put my key in the back of the door to give the bastard a taste of his own medicine, and then thought better of it. The game playing, like the marriage, was over.

I tried waiting up for him, but by midnight he had not appeared. Where the hell was he? I dispelled any frissons of concern. I was damned if I was going to ring him on his cell. As of 18:20 this evening, when I had put the phone down after talking to my father, Gary Goffrey without a D was no longer a concern of mine.

A glass of wine for Dutch courage turned into four glasses for-the-sake-of-it, and at one minute past midnight oblivion descended.

I slept heavily but with no dreams.

I awoke naturally, and quickly became aware that Gary was not beside me in the bed. I looked at the clock and then did a double-take. 08:30. My God, I had been out for eight and a half hours. I was due in the shop at 10:00.

Wondering where the hell my soon-to-be-ex-husband had got to, I scrambled out of bed. I heard noises coming from elsewhere in the apartment. Had he been to bed and got up again, or had he just got in? The bed seemed slept in on both sides, but that could have been me with my twisting and turning.

I showered, fuzzed up my short hair (it would do for today) and applied the minimum make-me-look-at-least-slightly-alive make-up.

Gary was at the kitchen table eating some cereal. "Morning, Angel Baby."

"Where were you last night?" My voice was cold.

"Didn't you see my note?"

There was no fucking note. Was he running out of ideas, were we back to the note thing again? I didn't respond.

"I was out with Clive," he explained. "I walked home. Wanted some air. Got in about one. Don't you remember, we talked?"

"No, we - " I bit my tongue then took a breath as I poured myself a glass of orange juice. "Gary," I said. "I don't want to be married to you any more."

He continued eating his *Fruit Loops*, as if I hadn't said anything. I watched him finish the last two spoonfuls, and then he stood up and quickly rinsed his bowl under hot water before the dregs got stuck to the side. I was standing, leaning against the work surface.

He smiled, polite, sweet, almost affectionate. "I'm sorry, Angel Baby, what did you say?"

I walked away from him. "I said I want a divorce." I looked back at him from the doorway.

He frowned, as if he couldn't comprehend what I was saying. "What?"

"Can I be any clearer? I want a divorce."

Confusion crawled across his face. His eyes welled, and then perfectly parallel tears ran down his cheeks. "Why?"

"Perhaps you've just answered your own question. The fact that you have to ask why."

"I don't understand..."

A part of me wanted to reach out to him, to touch him, to hold him. My husband.

"I'm late for work," I said. "We'll speak tonight."

58

The window was open when I came home that evening, which meant he was in. Every evening, even though I knew the lock would be blocked by his key in the other side, I had tried my key in the door. I had vowed never to give him the triumph of having me knock without trying to get into my own apartment first. So tonight I tried my key as usual, and was shocked when it slipped into the lock without blockage from the other side.

I was so stunned, I took the key out and put it back in again! Tentatively I turned it, hearing the door unlock. For the first time ever in my marriage, I had managed to gain entry in the evening when my husband was home without having to ask him to open the door. I was knocked off kilter – which was, of course, the whole intention. Another little psychological point for the male.

As soon as I went in, I could hear the loud, desperate sobs coming from the bedroom. Gary was on the bed in the classic foetal position, crying like a child.

Without preamble, I said "Sorry, Gary, but it's over." I walked across and put my bag on the dressing table.

He could hardly speak between the sobs. "But... but... you can't. We're... we're... married for life, remember?"

"That's just for fairytales," I sounded hard. I felt hard. I wanted to be hard.

"B – but what h-have I done?"

"You want a list? Give me a break. You know what you've done, what you've been doing for the last three years. You probably know more than I do. Trying to extort money from my father was the last straw."

"B- but it was for us. You're m- my Angel Baby!"

"Your Angel Baby is dead, Gary."

Something shot across his eyes. Then he said, "I love you."

"You love me?" I stood, hands on hips, next to the bed. "Love is not playing mind games, love is not dissing my friends, love is not cheating my father, love is not sponging off of me while you bring in a mere pittance and then keep it for yourself, love is not fucking me when you know I'm hurting."

"I- I thought you liked it."

I lowered my voice to a normal level. "How could I possibly like being hurt?"

His red-rimmed, swollen eyes looked up at me. The crying had dulled the green. There was no spark behind them – just emptiness. "Some people do."

"Not me."

He sighed a deep, deep sigh. Then something strange, something tangible happened. He straightened his body out of the foetal position, shook from head to foot and was then still. As if one spirit had left him and another had taken over. Instantly his eyes dried, and he smiled up at me. He moved his legs over the side and stood up off the bed. "If only you knew."

"If only I knew what?

"Nothing, Carly. You know absolutely nothing. You want a divorce? Fine. Now, if you'll excuse me, I've got work to do."

He walked passed me. Once again, he had managed to unsettle my soul. "Three weeks," I said, following him into the living room. "I want you out in three weeks."

He turned. "Okay." The green eyes stared at me "It's been... interesting, hasn't it?"

"Has it?"

"Carly," he took a step back towards me and then thought better of it.

I stood my ground, not saying anything.

He shrugged. "Okay." He turned, walked over and sat down at his computer.

I breathed a sigh of relief and offered up a silent prayer. Was that it? Was it all over?

Like hell it was.

I am still alive

Georgie sat hugging his knees, grinning broadly.

Oh, you're good Daddy. So, so good. Which meant you were bad.

She played along with it, just like you knew she would.

And she doesn't even know! She has no idea. The stupid bitch thinks it's her decision! The poor, deluded, manipulated imbecile.

She has no brains. Unlike you, Daddy. You are a genius.

But must we leave, Daddy?

Must I come in? Can I stay out and play a little longer....?

PART SIX

Climax

59

Never did he call me Angel Baby ever again. Not once. Although I hated the name, it gave me the creeps to think that he could turn it off just like that. He remained civil to me, quite pleasant in fact, but now that we were just two people living together rather than a husband and wife, he stayed out more or disappeared at odd times of the day.

Should we have been like this all along? Was it the marriage, rather than the relationship, that was a mistake?

I think not.

He came home one day from one of his little sojourns with a big bruise on his forearm. "How'd you get that?" I asked.

"Get what?"

"The bruise." I tapped my arm.

"What bruise – Oh! Goodness me. I don't know."

"Come on, Gary. A bruise that size, you're going to know how you got it."

"Don't know... Ah, I know. When I went out this morning, some man with a briefcase bumped into me. I didn't think anything of it at the time."

"A man with a briefcase," I sneered. Why could he never just give me a straight answer. Truth be told, I didn't even care how he got the fucking bruise. "Are you sure it wasn't the Bulgarian Secret Service stabbing you with a poisoned umbrella?"

He laughed. "Oh, Carly." Then the laugh fell from his face as if it had never been there. "Now you're being stupid."

60

Another evening, we were sitting watching the news (separate chairs, none of the entwined bodies of our early marriage), when suddenly he sprang forward. "Shit, my knee's sore."

I raised an eyebrow. "Not the man with the briefcase again?" My God, I should have been in vaudeville.

"Very funny." He rolled up the right leg of his jeans. There was a nasty looking graze on his knee.

"How did you do that?"

"I don't know." (I could have written that line, couldn't I?)

"Did you fall over? Are your jeans torn?"

He pulled the leg of the jeans back down again, feeling the cloth. "No, they're all right."

"So you must have had your jeans off or rolled up to graze your knee like that without tearing the cloth."

"Carly," he said, "if you can't say anything constructive, why don't you just shut up."

"And why don't you just fuck off," I retorted. "Two weeks and counting."

"Or what?"

"You either get out or get thrown out."

"Oooh!" He wiggled his fingers in front of my face. "Now I'm scared."

"Seriously, Gary. I want you out."

"And I want me out too. Don't worry, I'll be gone."

"Good." We were quiet for a minute, then I said "Do you want me to put some cream on that graze for you?"

He thought about it. "No, it's okay. It'll teach me a lesson. Lessons have to be learnt, Carly."

I said nothing more about it

The news finished at 22:30. As the weather girl (sorry, weather *person*) was again telling us in great detail about the weather we had already had that day, Gary stood up. "I'm just going to take the rubbish out."

"Leave it," I said. "It's raining. I'll take it out in the morning."

"No, no, I'll do it now."

To take the rubbish down to the bins out the front would take 30 seconds. Okay, say one minute with a sore knee.

It was ten minutes before Gary came back.

"You took your time," I said. "Where've you been for ten minutes?"

I thought he was going to say he'd bumped into one of the other occupants of the building and had been talking. "I slipped over in the rain," he said. "I was a bit dizzy. I was just sitting there on the step."

"You okay?"

"I am now, yes."

I looked him up and down. I took a breath to say something, then thought better of it. He was no concern of mine anymore.

Gary had said he had slipped over in the rain. Yet there wasn't a wet mark, there wasn't a scuff, on him.

61

He was being unusually nice to me the next morning. I was off on a job, then in the evening I was going out to dinner.

"Did I tell you I was going out to dinner with Clarke tonight?"

"Your brother? No, you didn't. Can I come?"

"No."

He looked at my big make-up case. "Where are you doing this job?"

"None of your business."

"I just thought I could help you with your stuff. That thing always looks so heavy."

"It is. Tools of the trade and all that. But I can manage, thanks."

I just didn't want this man to know where I was going, what I was doing, anything. The job was literally just up the road (a fashion shoot in Washington Square Park), but as far as he was concerned I wanted him to think I was far away. Otherwise he would turn up.

I thought of calling a taxi, but the walk would do me good. As I stepped out into the street, I was aware of Gary's eyes on me from the window. I crossed the road, turned the corner into MacDougal Street and was out of sight. Thank God the burning in my back stopped.

But the ringing in my purse started.

I looked at the caller ID on my cell. It was him.

I sighed as I answered. "Yes?"

"Carly, what time do you think you will be home?"

It was a timed modelling shoot; I knew the exact hours assigned. "I don't know, the job will take as long as it takes."

"Call me when you've finished and I can come and help you with your stuff."

"I don't need your help. I'll be home when I'm home."

Was he being concerned for me? It was not too long since my latest hospital incident, so perhaps he was trying to be the gentleman. But more likely he was up to something, that's why he wanted to know when I would return.

I heard nothing further from him during the day, and the shoot finished at 15:00. By 15:30 I was walking back along Minetta Lane, the apartment in sight.

As I came towards the building, I saw a woman coming down the front steps. Who was that? I had never seen her before. Perhaps someone had had a visitor.

I looked carefully as she walked off in the opposite direction. She was wearing a short beige rainmac over what must have been an even shorter skirt because I could not see it. She was holding a plastic *Wal-Mart* carrier bag in her arms, as if it contained something precious.

The platinum blonde hair was long and stiff. Unnatural. Like a wig. And the legs, although long and slender, were distinctly masculine, as was the gait as she walked away. I knew all the residents of the building, and I couldn't imaging any of them entertaining a transvestite in the middle of the afternoon – except perhaps one.

One who was very eager that morning to know what time his soon-to-be-ex-wife would be returning home…

I reached the front stairs and looked up. The window was open, which meant he was in.

I lugged my big make-up box and my bag up the two floors to our front door. I tried my key in the lock – to find his key was back in the other side. I thought we'd finished with all that.

I tapped on the door. No reply. I knocked louder. Nothing.

Oh, for Christ's sake.

Thumping loudly on the door, I shouted "Gary! It's me." Was he locking me out of my own home now that I had asked him for a divorce? I should have seen this coming. "Gary! I know you're in there!"

Nothing.

The stairway was quiet, probably everyone else in the building was still at work. No one had come to see what the shouting was about. In fact, it was so quiet it was eerie.

I was deciding what to do when I heard something.

"Hee, hee, hee, hee, hee."

A little boy's voice. A naughty little boy's voice. An evil little boy's voice.

A shiver ran down my spine. You bastard, I should have expected the games to intensify now you'd got your marching orders. Well, Mama wasn't playing.

I began kicking and punching the door. "Let me in, you bastard. Gary, I know you're there."

"Hee, hee, hee, hee, hee."

"Open the fucking door!"

The giggling stopped. I expected to hear his key turn in the lock, but nothing happened. "Gary?"

I left my bags there and went back down to the front door, being careful to keep it held open. I pushed our bell and held my finger on it. It was a full thirty seconds before the front door catch was released from the entry phone in the apartment.

I ran back upstairs, expecting to see him standing in the doorway. He wasn't there, but the apartment door had been opened just a tad. Enough to let me know I could get in - but not enough for me to see inside, to see if anybody was waiting behind the door.

Quietly, cautiously, I pushed the door open with my index finger. Noiselessly it swung back.

No one there.

The bathroom door was just beyond the small vestibule. I opened it and poked my head in.

No one there.

The living room door on my left was open. I pushed it slightly and there was a distinct creak. The room was beginning to get dark as night fell outside. There were no lights on.

But there was no one there.

On the other side of the living room was the bedroom door, shut tight.

When watching horror movies, I would scoff scornfully at the heroine as she went deeper and deeper into a scary building, knowing that danger was lurking nearby. So unreal, I would mock; all human instinct would make her turn tail and run out of there. So what did I do now? I walked quietly over to the bedroom door and pushed it.

The door opened about a foot. It was dark inside, as if the curtains were drawn. It was very still. Not a sound came from within. Time to take my own advice.

Gently I closed the door. Then on swift tiptoe I hightailed it out of the apartment and back onto the stairs.

Fuck.

Fuck, fuck, fuck.

What the hell was I to do? Should I knock on other doors? Nobody had come out when I was shouting and thumping on the door a few minutes ago.

I bent forward and rummaged in my bag, finding my cell. I needed the advice of a friend. The scroll stopped at Jenny. She would do nicely.

It seemed to take ages to connect. Come on, come on, come on.

Then Jenny answered.

"Jenny!" I tried to keep my voice low.

Jenny told me she wasn't available but if I left a message she would call me back.

Shinola.

Should I call someone else? Should I call the police? What could I say? I want to get into my apartment but my husband is acting really strange – yes, the door is open; yes, I can get in.

Phone in my hand, I went back downstairs and pressed the doorbell again. Another thirty seconds with my finger on the button. Then the click as the catch released again.

I had taken one step back towards the stairs when my cell rang and nearly scared the living shit out of me (actually, I think it did, but you don't want to know that). It was him.

"Gary?"

"Hi Babe – Carly. Where are you? I've opened the door for you."

Okay, fine, for the thousandth time I'll play along. "Thanks. I'm coming now."

"What are you doing down there? Your stuff's up here outside the door."

I shut my phone without replying.

He was standing in the doorway. His right hand was down by his side, clenched as if he had something in it. He watched as I walked up the stairs. "Did you have a nice day?" he asked solicitously.

"Fine." I didn't want him to see that I had clocked his hand, but I needed to know what was in it before I took another step. "Gary, could you take my make-up box in for me?" I nodded to the floor.

He was the complete gentleman. "Sure." He picked it up. There was nothing in his hand.

Back inside, the living room light was now on and his computer screen was active. The bedroom door was noticeably closed again. Something told me that I didn't want to go in there. I was meeting my brother, I could go as I was, my make-up was here with me.

"So, tell me about your day." The ever-so-normal Gary sat down at his keyboard.

"Why don't you cut the crap and tell me why you didn't answer the fucking door."

A smile. "I don't know what you're talking about." So reasonable, so calm. So normal. "I didn't hear anything."

"Didn't hear anything what? Didn't hear me calling you? Didn't hear me trying to kick the door in? And I heard you laughing."

He was nodding. "The TV must have been up too loud."

"Gary, the TV's not even on!"

"Well, I don't know what you're talking about. Anyway, I was on the phone to somebody in London."

"Who?"

"A photographer. I've set up an interview with him."

"In London?"

"Yep."

"You're going away?"

"Yep."

"When?"

"Soon."

Was this it? Was my chance going to be presented to me? Or was this another little game?

Later, when I returned from a great evening with my brother Clarke, Gary was already in bed. Unheard of. And asleep. Even more unheard of.

The piquant smell in the bedroom indicated that Gary had had sex while I'd been out. I presumed it was with his right hand.

Or maybe it was with a platinum blonde transvestite.

62

I just didn't want to be around this man.

The next night was a Saturday – and I stayed out all the night. No, I wasn't up to anything, I was just drinking with a gang of friends, and then we all crashed in someone's front room.

From about 22:30 the previous evening, Gary had been trying to contact me. After three calls in half an hour – all of which I ignored - the amusement wore off and I turned off my phone. When I put it on again at 06:30 the next morning I had no less than thirty-two missed calls and thirty-three texts. The calls had been made precisely at every fifteen minutes during the night, followed by a text, always the same three word message: *Where are you?*

I arrived back at the apartment at 08:00 on Sunday morning. I was due in work at MAC at 11:00.

His key in the door, me thumping on it.

He seemed genuinely bleary-eyed when he opened the door, but he wasn't fooling me that he'd been up all night worried. I knew with his skills he could quite easily have programmed his computer to ring me and send the messages.

"Carly, darling, where have you been?" His voice was sincere, concerned, relieved and almost breaking.

"Just out with the gang."

"I've been so worried about you." He followed me into the kitchen. Thank God there was coffee in the pot. "I've called your friends. And the police."

I stopped. "What?"

"You even made me call the police."

"What the hell did you do that for? I've just been out for the night. And we're not husband and wife anymore, remember?"

"Oh but we are."

"On paper only, Gary," I poured coffee into my mug. "I've got to go and have a shower and get ready for work – yes, I'm going out again, get used to it. Who did you call out of my friends?"

"Tara and Selma." My MAC managers.

"Well, I suggest you call them back and tell them I'm okay."

A shower can do wonders for a girl's spirit. I closed my eyes as the water made tactile the odours of booze and cigarettes (and the odour of a girl who has been out all the night) and swirled them away down the drain. It was a much improved Carly who re-entered the battlefield an hour later, freshly made-up and ready for the day, albeit with disobedient eyelids that were pleading for proper sleep.

"Did you call everybody?" I asked.

He was on the computer. What a surprise. He didn't turn round. "Yes."

"Have you called them all?"

"Yes, I've called them all."

"Good."

At the doorway, I turned back to look at him. "Gary?"

For a moment I thought he hadn't heard me. Then he said, "Mm?"

"We're separated. We might still live together, but we're not a couple anymore. You will have to get used to it."

He carried on typing. "I was worried about you."

"Don't be. I'm no longer your concern. As you are no longer

any concern of mine."

"That sounds cruel."

"That sounds real."

Then, as I turned to leave, he said words which still send a chill through me today.

"Be careful. Anything could happen to you."

63

Being a Sunday, it was pleasant to walk up the Avenue of the Americas without the hell of the weekday traffic. I was in work in fifteen minutes. The shop wasn't open for another ten minutes, but Tara was already inside. When she saw who was knocking on the glass door, her face screwed up and she dashed over to let me in.

"Carly!"

"Hi Tara, what's wrong? Hey!" She was crying.

"I've been so worried about you."

"What do you mean?"

"Your husband phoned me at six this morning. Said you'd gone missing, he didn't know where you were."

"Yes, and then he called you at eight to tell you I'd come back in."

"No," she sniffed. "No, he didn't."

"What? Oh God, Tara," I put my arms around her shoulders as we walked behind the fixtures to her little office. "I'm so, so sorry. I thought he'd rung you. He told me he did."

While Tara composed herself – and I felt like shit for putting her through this – I phoned Selma.

Immediately she heard my voice, she said "Carly, thank God you're okay."

"Gary didn't call you, did he?"

"Yes, he did! That's how I knew you were missing."

"No, I mean he didn't call you back. To tell you I was okay."

"No, he just called the once."

After I had calmed both of my friends, I dragged out the dusty old local phone book from a drawer, looked up the number and phoned the 6th Precinct police at West 10th Street.

I told them who I was, that my husband had reported me missing that morning, that it was all a big mistake, I had just stayed out the night, I was okay.

I heard the policeman tapping on a keyboard. Then there was a pause. He seemed uncertain. "Did your husband call this precinct, ma'm?"

"Well, I presume he would have done. I don't think he would have called 911."

"We have no record of any missing persons report, ma'm."

Why hadn't I guessed that? "Oh. He said he reported me as missing."

"There's nothing on the database, ma'm."

"Well, okay, sorry to have wasted your time."

"That is an offence, ma'm. You wouldn't want to be doing that, would you?"

"What?"

"Wasting police time."

"Of course not. He told me he'd phoned you. Probably just wanted to scare me, that's all. Sorry."

"I've noted the details anyway, Mrs Goffrey."

"Actually, you know officer, I'm damn glad you have." Because I think I may be needing you again. "Thank you."

64

Four days until the Memorial Day weekend.

I was taking four days vacation and I had planned to spend at least one night with my friend Terry and her kids in the Upper West Side. Not too far away – perhaps an hour for those damn crows – but far enough away from the prying eyes and mind games of Mr Gary Goffrey.

But after the débâcle with Tara and Selma, I decided to let him know where I was going. "I'm going away for the weekend. I'll be at Terry's."

He feigned disinterest. "Okay, fine."

"I've left her number next to the phone, but I don't want you ringing me unless the earth stops spinning."

"Okay, fine."

Three days until the Memorial Day weekend.

I sat on the edge of the couch, watching *Good Morning America* and eating a yoghurt before going off to work.

He came in with a slice of toast and coffee. "Hi."

"Hi."

"What are you doing this weekend? It's Memorial Day."

I didn't take my eyes off the television. "I told you I'm going to stay with my friend Terry."

"Oh, which friend's that then?" He strolled across and settled himself down in front of the computer, like a pilot climbing into his cockpit.

"Terry? Upper West Side?" I turned off the TV with the remote and stood up, empty yoghurt pot in hand.

As I went into the kitchen, he said "You'd best give me her number in case I need to get hold of you."

"I gave it to you yesterday."

"Give it to me again, will you?"

Two days until the Memorial Day weekend.

It had been a busy day at the shop, and consequently I was in no mood for it when I got home.

As he let me into the apartment, he asked chirpily "What are we going to do this weekend?"

"We? We are going to do nothing, Gary. Can't you get it into your head that the marriage is over? I'm going to spend time with my friend."

He followed me into the bedroom. "What friend?"

I dropped my bag onto the bed. "You know, I used to think you were cunning. But maybe you're just stupid."

"What friend?"

I undid my skirt and let it drop to the floor. My black tights and G-string seemed not to interest him. "Gary. Just fuck off."

One day until the Memorial Day weekend.

The shop would be open over the holiday, of course, but I had the days off. A nice, long weekend. It was a tired but happy Carly that came home that evening.

I ate then went into the living room and turned on the TV. You can guess where he was. He beavered away without a word, tip-tappy-tap-tap, for some twenty minutes while I watched 24 (and fantasised about Jack Bauer coming to my rescue).

As the cliffhanging split screen and closing clock countdown announced the end of the programme, he turned. The green eyes were darker than usual. The grin was pure malice. Without preamble, he said "I've got a surprise for you. I've bought you a present."

I raised my eyebrows. "It's a bit late for presents, Gary."

"No, I really want you to have this one."

I expected him to produce a patriotic T-shirt from somewhere, or maybe a stars and stripes pen or something. Or anything. What did he do? He turned back around and continued with his work, without another word.

Half an hour (and one whole episode of *Frasier*) later, he finished what he was doing with a flourish and turned around.

"Did I tell you I bought you a present?"

Okay, round two begins. Seconds out, *ding ding.*

"Yes you did, Gary. I'm not interested." I kept my gaze on the opening credits of *Las Vegas.*

"I'd really like you to see this present, I took particular care in choosing it for you." He had the gleefulness of a child.

"You can take all the care in the world you want, I don't want your present."

Would you believe that this went on intermittently for an hour and a half? Making me lose my concentration on *Las Vegas* and completely miss the late news.

As some gamin was telling me that the Memorial Day weekend was going to be fine with clear skies but with perhaps a chance of torrential thunderstorms, I lost my patience.

"Okay, fine, show me the damn present. Then you can fuck off and leave me alone for the rest of the night, if you don't mind."

He stood up. "You have to go into the kitchen."

"Oh really? Right, what is it? Another saucepan or something?"

"Come." He stretched out his hand but I didn't take it.

From the cutlery drawer, he produced a long, flat box.

Hadn't we been here before? I was glad I had stayed in the doorway.

Leaving the box to one side, he took out the chopping knife he had bought me just after we were married (the one that was so good with bones) and carefully laid it on the work surface. Then he opened the box and took out my new 'present': a twelve inch carving knife. Gently he laid it in perfect symmetry with the chopping knife.

"There! What do you think of that? It's a beautiful piece of artwork, isn't it?"

"It's just a knife, Gary."

"Not just a knife, Carly. This is Japanese." He picked it up, weighing it in his hand. "Perfect. Look at that, it's even got a finger rest where you grip it."

"How very thoughtful of them."

"So you can cut exactly where you want to cut. Actually," he looked slightly naughty, "I know I bought this for you, but I need it too."

"Really? What do you need it for?"

He didn't repress his excitement. "Because I need to be able to cut and chop everything – and anything. And with both of these, I can! But," he frowned, "if I were you I wouldn't get too close to this knife, because you just might have an accident."

I stiffened, gripping the door frame.

"Because after all," he sounded so reasonable, "you are clumsy."

"I – I'm not clumsy at all."

"Oh yes, you are." The green eyes were positively gleaming as he looked down at the two knives.

I had flashbacks of me dropping things, suddenly losing my balance, tipping over my drinks... Maybe he was right, maybe I was clumsy.

"Let's bring them to perfection!" he gleamed.

"W- what?"

From the cupboard under the sink, he brought out one of his

two knife sharpeners. I was transfixed as he slid the new knife through it, once, twice, three times. I wondered if that sound it made on metal was the same as the one it would make on bone.

He lifted it up to his face, running his finger along the edge. For a moment I thought he was going to kiss it. His breath caused condensation on the blade. "Oh, that's like paper. Paper thin, that is."

"What did you sharpen it for?" I asked, with a braveness I did not feel. "It's not like you'll be cutting meat with it, we don't eat meat. Got a particularly tough piece of garlic, have you?"

He smiled at me tolerantly. "You never know when I might need it."

The sudden blast of adrenaline through my system made me want to retch. I took two paces forward and snatched up the chopping knife.

"That one won't do you any good," he said conversationally. "It's not as sharp as this one."

Somehow my legs carried me back into the living room. Trying to scare me, were you, you bastard? Well, you had succeeded. But I wasn't going to let you know that. Now I was armed too. Want to make something of it?

I heard the carving knife being put back into the drawer, and then he strolled in and went back on the computer. I sat on the couch, the chopping knife tucked down the edge of the cushion, touching my hand.

Half an hour and one documentary on something I didn't take in later, he started to giggle. The naughty little boy was here again. He slipped into the kitchen and then came back into the living room with the new knife. Instinctively I moved my hand down to touch the blade next to me.

Gently, oh so gently, he placed his knife next to the computer, absentmindedly stroking it as he stared at whatever it was he had written on the screen.

A voice in my head was urging me to do it. Do it, Carly, do it. Pre-emptive self-defence. Go on, do it.

I gripped my knife and pushed myself forward onto the edge of the couch.

I stood up, knife in hand, staring at the back of his head.

"It is beautiful, isn't it?" he said without turning. It was as if he was presenting his back to me and daring me. Had he heard me stand up?

I looked down at the knife in my hand and imagined it covered with his blood, imagined the blood over my hand and up my arm, hot, maybe even steaming. I saw his head split open and the pink entrails of his brain spilling out.

Raising the knife, I took one slow step towards him...

Then he turned around, grinning. "Absolutely beautiful." Picking up a pencil, he began to sketch the knife on his notepad. "You okay, Carly? You look a bit... pale. Perhaps you should go to bed."

I jolted back to reality. As I lowered my arm, I felt the demon leave me as quickly as it had entered me. Had I really been about to murder him? Had Gary wanted me to try to murder him?

This would not be a good night, I thought, to go to bed with this lunatic. I sighed and turned away, back to my chair.

Come midnight, I could see he was getting ready to close down. I reached forward and took out an old Richard Pryor DVD from the shelf under the coffee table. "Gary, you've been working too hard. Come and watch Richard Pryor."

"A dead comedian? I don't think so. I'm tired, I'm going to turn in."

"Okay. Don't mind if I stay up and watch it, do you?"

"Why should I?"

I watched Richard Pryor, I watched Chris Rock, I could have watched *War and Peace* and the Director's Cut of *Dances With Wolves*. I stayed in that living room all night. Which was daft really. Because at two o'clock I fell unconscious and the next thing I knew it was nearly seven in the morning. Had he wanted to do anything to me, he had had five hours to do it.

But I was intact, if a little stiff, when I heard him coming out of the bedroom.

"You been there all night?" He walked past me to the kitchen.

"God, I must have nodded off," I shook my head. "What time is it? Seven? I need to pack my things."

"Why? You going away somewhere?"

Wham. Thank you, Gary. First one of the day to you.

"Terry's. You know I am."

I got myself ready, and at 08:00 I opened the front door. "Right, I'm off to Terry's now. I'll be back Sunday night."

He didn't turn around. "Who's Terry?"

I slammed the door behind me as I walked out.

Downstairs, out in the street, I told myself not to do it. But I did. I looked up.

And there at the window was the little boy with the sad face, waving goodbye to me.

65

Terry's children were like any others. A present each from Auntie Carly, a couple of Memorial Day chocolate bars (the price of those things!) and I had paid my Danegeld. They went off contented, to play with their X-Box or whatever kids do nowadays.

I sat in Terry's kitchen, drinking her excellent coffee and apologising for my early arrival. She was a friend, as always. "That's no problem, Carls. Providing you don't mind the state of the place."

"Mind? My God, this is heaven. Normality."

"You been having problems again?"

"And then some. You know what he's like, Tair. But… I don't know. He has a way of making me think it's me, that I'm the one going mad."

"But you're not."

"Of course not. He's just so damn… clever. But recently he's been different. We seem to be going one step further than we've ever been, and I don't know where it will end. Last night was surreal."

"Want to tell me about it?"

"Well, it - "

"Hold on!" she interrupted. "I've got a surprise for you."

I stiffened involuntarily. I had heard those same words last night. But this was my friend. This was Terry.

"What?" Keep it light, Carly, don't lose it.

"Helena is coming round later and I'm cooking us all lunch. Perhaps the three witches from Macbeth can talk about it then!"

"Hels? That's brilliant! God, it's been ages since I've seen her."

"So I'll just check on the brats, then you can help me chop the vegetables. And you can give me a little preview of what's been happening. See those three bottles of red wine on the side?"

"Yep."

"Open all of them, will you?"

Terry had gotten her preview, but she was as aghast as Helena when, over vegetable lasagne and three bottles of Italian Barolo, I told them all the gruesome details of my marriage, of my life.

"You've kept this all very quiet," commented Terry. "I had no idea. I knew he always seemed a bit *strange*, anti-social if you like. But I never thought... Why haven't you told us this before?"

"I was never certain whether it was just me. Was I imagining it? I married him very quickly. I thought I was in love. Despite everybody telling me to be careful. I suppose I wanted everybody to see that I *had* made the right choice." I couldn't stop the sob.

Helena reached out and touched my hand. "Carly, you can't go back. This guy is a lunatic. The knife thing is scary. He could do something to you."

"Or I could do something to him – which is even scarier. Hels, I was this much - " I held my hands apart about two feet, " – this much away from putting a knife into his head. I just don't know what's happening to me."

"Well, it's over. Whatever is happening, it's over."

"But I have to go back, he's expecting me. And it won't look good for the divorce."

"Then we'll make up a story. You can't go back alone."

The story was that Helena had asked me to help her on a shoot she was doing in the Hamptons. Both my friends would accompany me back to the apartment on Sunday night. Terry would stay outside in her car, engine running. Helena would come inside with me while I collected everything I could carry.

Good cloak and dagger stuff, right?

I called Gary on the Sunday, telling him about the fictitious job and that I wouldn't be back fully until Tuesday night, but that I would need to pop back and get some clean panties and things. "Please take the key out of the door if you are in so that I won't disturb you."

"Okay, whatever."

Naturally the key was still in the lock, but Gary's face fell as he saw Helena standing there with me. Muttering an unfelt "Thanks," I pushed past him and went straight through the living room into the bedroom. I could hear Helena engaging him in conversation outside.

Grabbing a holdall (one of many I had picked up on my freelance jobs, 'Shoot Loot' we called them), I opened my drawer and began to pile stuff into it. Gary's drawer was poking out a little bit where it had not been closed tight, and without thinking I opened it to see if there was any of my stuff in there, what with his predilection for wearing my clothes.

All the stuff in there was his. Including his passport. Thinking several chess moves ahead, without hesitation I picked it up and slipped it into my back pocket.

"Where are you going?"

I jumped. Gary was standing in the doorway, Helena looking concerned behind me. Had he seen me pocket the passport?

"I told you. The Hamptons."

"It's a great opportunity for her," said Helena from behind, diverting his attention. "The Food Network. The *Barefoot Contessa*. Ina Garten?"

"A garden?"

"Food and friends. Only the best make-up artists are used. You must have heard of it."

"No." He turned back to look at me. "When will you be back?"

"Tuesday night." Why did I have the feeling that he knew I was lying?

I zipped up my holdall and pushed past him.

Down in the street, I said to Helena "Look up, he'll be waving from the damn window."

Surreptitiously as she got into the car, Hels looked up. The little boy was there, waving us goodbye.

Terry slipped the car into drive and we shot off towards 6th Avenue.

66

I stayed with Helena that night, dossing on the couch in her small apartment in Chelsea. We drank, we smoked, we talked,

As I slipped off my jeans prior to settling down under the quilt she had given me, Gary's Australian passport fell out onto the floor. Helena had gone to bed and it was still and quiet in the apartment.

I picked it up. Why had I taken this? It was an impetuous, spur-of-the-moment thing. He said he was going to London, I should have left it. Now he couldn't get out of the country – and my God did I want him to do that. Get out and never come back. I should return it.

The passport was old and well worn. Idly I flicked through it. There were quite a few entry and exit stamps from various countries: The Philippines, Japan, even Vietnam. Then one or two in the northern hemisphere when he was en route to the States.

Something rather grand and formal caught my eye. It was a residency visa. From US Immigration.

How the hell had he got that? I had never written the second letter or had a second interview with Immigration. I had mentioned it to Gary that it was strange they had never contacted me again after eighteen months like they had said they would, but he had shrugged it off saying perhaps they had forgotten, there were thousands of people wanting residency in the USA, the land where the streets were paved with gold.

I would confront him about it next time I saw him.

In the back of the passport, a much younger Gary stared wistfully out at me, the green eyes noticeable even in the passport photograph. He had long hair, which made me giggle.

But then the smile was instantly wiped off my face.

Something in the detail next to the picture made me double-take. I looked and looked again.

Another lie. It was typical Gary really, perhaps I should have guessed it. But I had never realised.

The man whose passport I was holding, whom I had been married to for over three years, was not Gary Goffrey.

Gary Goffrey did not exist.

His name was George.

George Michael Goffrey.

I'll pick up sticks

Georgie stood in the middle of the living room. One hand was playing with his winkie, the other held a glass of whisky.

Daddy wasn't here. Daddy was going to be gone for a few days, at least until Tuesday. Before he left, Daddy had taken him to the bathroom. He had looked at him in the mirror and softly, gently, he had told him that they would be moving soon. Time to pick up sticks and go.

Again, Daddy? But why? We had been here a long time this time. Did we have to go? Couldn't we settle down?

No, son, no. Things are coming to a head again. It's best all round if we move on.

Then Daddy had left. Georgie was here in the apartment on his own. Georgie could do whatever he liked.

He took his hand off his winkie and staggered over to the computer. His right ankle buckled and he almost fell. Some whisky sloshed from his glass. How did women wear these damned high heels?

He looked down at his smooth, shaved legs. At Mommy's black G-string that could not contain his equipment. At the black suspenders and stockings. At the bra that Daddy had bought for him because Mommy's titties were too small and her bra wouldn't even fit over his shoulders.

He liked what he saw.

Reaching out, he picked up the vial from the table, snapped off the top, and held it under his nose...

67

Naturally I did not return on Tuesday night. It was never my intention that I should. I spent two nights with Helena, and then moved on to stay with Terry.

Having children around took a bit of getting used to, but it was heaven. It was normality.

Gary had not phoned me, which was unusual. Normally I would be plagued with phone calls, even if I was out for just an evening. For me to be out for several days and not be hounded was unheard of.

Or was this another game. Were we in a war of attrition? See who would contact the other first?

The war ended the next Sunday afternoon, a full week after I had gone away. I was working in the MAC shop in Christopher Street when he called.

"Hello, Carly, where are you?" It was as if I'd gone up the road for a quart of milk and was late coming back.

I wasn't going to beat about the bush (his or anybody else's). "Gary, you know I'm never coming back to you."

"Oh?"

"You are really weird."

Silence.

"Do you understand me?"

"Yep."

"From now on I don't want you coming anywhere near me. Or my friends or my family. Do you understand?"

"Okay."

"You need to get out of that apartment. It's mine, the lease is in my name. My money pays for it. If you don't get out, I'll have you thrown out."

"Have you got my passport?"

I said nothing for a moment. Then I admitted, "Yes. Yes, I do."

"What are you doing with it? I want it back?"

"You can't have it back. Not until you tell me how you got residency."

"Because you wrote a letter to Immigration."

"No, I didn't, not at all."

"Yes, you did."

"I didn't." Then I corrected myself. "Well, yes, I did. One directly after we got married. They said they would contact me again in eighteen months, that I would be asked to submit both our passports and bills from a residence that we were both named on, and I would have to be interviewed and write a personal letter that I was still satisfied with the marriage and was still happy living with you."

"You did that."

"I never did!"

"Obviously you did. How else would I have got residence? It's another of your memory lapses."

Fuck you, Gary. Fuck you, fuck you, fuck you. I did not. I had not.

"Anyway, I'm going to need my passport back."

I was confused. "Really? Why?"

"I have to go to France to interview Karl Lagerfeld."

"Oh, do you now? Is this before or after London?"

"Before. Why don't you come by the apartment tonight and drop it off?"

"I don't think I'm going to be doing any such thing, am I? I think you are really dangerous."

"Me? I'm dangerous?"

"Good of you to admit it."

"Very funny. You always were a wag, Carly."

"And you always were a bastard, Gary."

"You know what? I've had it with you, you mad bitch. You're the dangerous one, not me. Keep the passport, if you like it so much. That won't stop me doing what I have to do."

"What do you mean?"

A beat, and then he said "You'll find out."

68

"I need to get back there to get the rest of my things out." Helena, Terry and I were sitting at our favourite table in Julius' Restaurant. "But I think that maniac's going to do something. I'm worried."

"I think it's about time you called the police." Terry popped a piece of cheese into her mouth and then took a swig of her white wine.

"And tell them what?" I asked. "That I've been married to this man for three years. That he constantly plays head games with me? That I've supposedly done things I can't remember doing?"

"But you haven't done things."

"But what if he can prove that I did? What if there is a second letter signed by me to Immigration? What if I did go for a second interview and I can't remember?"

Helena reached out and touched my arm. "Carly, you didn't. He's lying."

"Or," said Terry, "it wasn't you."

We both looked at her, shocked. "You mean...?"

"It could have been someone else. He could have got someone else to pretend they were you."

"He wouldn't..." A subliminal cut of a platinum blonde wig

flashed through my mind.

Terry went on. "And what about the cuts and bruises on your body?"

"I don't know how I got them. I have no proof whatsoever that he did them."

"And the illnesses?"

"He could get a thousand witnesses to testify that I was a sickly child."

"A sickness that just happened to return when you met him?"

I wiped my hands down my face. "But can you see what I mean? There's nothing tangible. Maybe everything is psychosomatic. Maybe it is me."

"Or maybe," said Terry, "he is just a very clever person."

I huffed. "Or maybe just fucking evil. But what do I say if I go to the police? I don't like my husband, please come and protect me while I get a fresh change of panties from my apartment? They won't come with me."

Helena was nodding. "But," she said, "does he know that?"

Both Terry and I turned our heads to look at our smiling friend.

69

"Gary, it's me." I was walking down 6th Avenue so that he could hear I was somewhere outside. "I've just been to the police. I'm coming back to the apartment, and the police are coming with me."

"*What?*"

"I don't want to be on my own with you anymore. You are a very dangerous man."

"What on earth are you saying?"

"I need to get some more of my things. It's up to you if you want to be there when the police come."

"No. No, I don't want to be."

"Okay, fine. Perhaps you'd best leave the house for a few hours then. You've got thirty minutes until we arrive."

It would never work, would it? But it seemed that it had.

Terry, Helena and I pulled up in the car a little way along from the building. Up on the first floor, all the windows were closed. A good sign.

Terry stayed in the car, à la getaway driver, and Hels and I went upstairs. My key went into the lock, and I opened the door.

"Gary?"

Nothing. I breathed a sigh of relief, but I motioned Hels to stay quiet just in case.

"Gary?"

In the living room, the computer was off. The kitchen door was open, and there was no one in there. On the other side of the living room, the bedroom door was ajar. I pushed it open and peeked in.

No one.

Helena could see the relief on my face, and then we both laughed. "It worked," I said.

It felt strange to be back in the apartment after a week away. There seemed to be something subtly different about the place, but I could not put my finger on it. The furniture was still the same, the blasted computer was still over there by the window, but there was just something... something...

That was it, it was the *atmosphere*. This was one of the very few times in the last three years when I had not been in the apartment at the same time as Mr Gary – make that George – Goffrey (and please put a D in if you like, I really don't give a shit). When he was here, there was an atmosphere of tension, almost of malevolence, in the place. Now he was not here, the structure of the building could relax. The atmosphere was... I wanted to think it was calming. It was not. It was dead.

I asked, "Hels, can you get anything?"

She was studying the photography magazines on the coffee table. "Sure. What would you like me to get?"

"No, I mean in this place. Do you *feel* anything?"

"Yes, I do - I feel we should get your things and go."

I nodded. "You're right." I went into the bedroom. Then I called, "Come and look at this."

Over his side of the bed were two large boxes. "Looks like he's packing," I said as my friend came in. "Excellent." I flipped open the top box. Inside it was packed with CD ROMs. "It's all his computer discs." There were probably 150 of them in the two boxes. They were all numbered, but there was nothing to indicate what was on them. The top one in this box was number 27.

Quickly I gathered some more of my clothes into another one of my bags. Halfway back across the living room, I stopped. "Mustn't forget this." I pulled the passport of George Goffrey from my pocket and threw it on the coffee table, then I continued on into the kitchen.

Things had been moved around in here. In the cupboard, the cans and packets of food were rearranged. And right in the front was a small box with *Prozac* printed on it. How bizarre.

The cupboard under the sink had been rearranged as well. I noticed an unfamiliar small plastic container behind the bleach bottle. I pulled it out.

Weed killer.

Three-quarters empty (okay, a quarter full if you'd prefer). "Hels, look." I held up the bottle. "Why would he have weed killer in the house when we don't even have a plant?"

Helena grimaced. "I couldn't tell you."

"Perhaps we really should have brought the police with us."

"Perhaps we really should get out of here."

"You're right."

I paused to look back into the apartment as I was closing the front door. *He* was packing to leave. *I* had already taken a lot of my clothes.

But I had the feeling that this was not over.

Maybe, I thought, it was only just beginning.

70

I called him the next evening, after the shop had closed.

"Thanks for being out yesterday."

"I didn't want to cause a fuss. What did you tell the police to get them to come with you?"

"The truth. Simply that I was afraid you might do something."

"You told them you're afraid of me?"

"No, I said I was afraid you might do something. There is a difference. I see you're packing."

"I've just been rearranging a few things."

"You need to go. You know you've got under two weeks now."

"Until?"

"Until I have you thrown out. I'm going to Washington for ten days - "

"What for?"

"Do you remember that job I told you about a few weeks ago? With *Jerry Bruckheimer Productions.*"

"You never told me."

"Shut up. You can't help yourself, can you? I told you about it. When I come back, I want to come back to my apartment. And I don't want you in it. Hear me?"

"I hear you."

"Right."

"Goodbye, Carly."

I put the phone down.

I'll still search for heaven

Georgie sat watching Daddy's reflection in the mirror. Daddy hadn't bothered with him today. Daddy was too busy packing, getting out.

Georgie had come to terms with the fact that they were moving on again. It was a pity, but Daddy was right – it was time.

Time to go. Time to continue the search for heaven elsewhere.

It was all that bitch's fault. Bitch Mommy. Bitch, bitch Mommy. And we had been having such fun as well! More fun than Mommy knew. But she would find out. Soon now.

And would she be in for a shock!

Surprise, surprise, Mommy! You couldn't have guessed it in a million years, could you?

A genius? Too fucking right I am.

Looking smug, Georgie walked over and began to seal the boxes of CD ROMs.

Helping Daddy.

PART SEVEN

The investigation

71

Ten days away. Ten days of work, but ten days of not having to worry about coming home to a psychopath in the evenings. So what did I do? I worried.

There were no phone calls from him the first day. None the second. None the third. By the fourth day I was wondering what he was getting up to. It was so unlike him not to call, to pester, to check on me.

So I phoned him.

From day five until day ten, I phoned him twice a day. And all I ever got was his voicemail. The first couple of times I left messages, asking him to phone me to let me know how he was getting on, when he would be moving out. The last few times I said nothing at all, but he would know it was me by the *Missed Calls* facility.

Perhaps he *had* moved out? Perhaps he had gone? Would that be too much to ask? I toyed with the idea of giving Jacqui a ring and asking her to go round to have a look, but that would have been unfair. And if he was still there, it might have been putting my friend in danger.

I thought I would find out soon enough what was going on, on my return to New York.

I didn't expect to find out on the train.

The 2100 Acela Express train was an hour into the nearly 3 hour journey from Washington Union Station to New York Penn. My book, the latest from a thriller writer friend of mine, was open on my lap. My mouth was open on my chest. How long had I been asleep? Probably a good half an hour. My cellphone woke me.

It said *Withheld Number*. Was this him doing the old *67 trick? Should I ignore it? My ring tone (*Chain Reaction*) was attracting glances from my fellow passengers, so I opened the phone.

"Hello?"

"Hello, is that Mrs Godfrey?" It was a male voice, deep and authoritative.

"Who's calling?"

"This is the New York City Police Department. This is Mrs Godfrey?"

"Goffrey, yes. Without a D."

"Are you all right, Mrs Goffrey?"

"I'm sorry?"

"Are you all right?"

"Yes, why wouldn't I be?"

"We've been round to your apartment. We could get no reply."

"Why did you go round to my apartment? Sorry – I'm confused. And how did you get my cellphone number?"

"We'd best not explain it on the phone, ma'm. Where are you now?"

"On a train. From Washington to Penn."

"And you intend going home?"

"Of course."

"It might be best if we came with you."

"Has something happened? Is there something you're not telling me?"

"We'll explain it when we see you, ma'm. We'll meet the

train."

"My friend is meeting me."

"We'll meet you too. Do you know what time you'll arrive?"

"Er... probably in two hours or just under."

"Right, we'll be there."

"How will I know you? I take it you won't be in uniform."

"Don't worry, ma'm. We'll know you."

I sat with my phone in my hand, staring out of the train window. The Pennsylvania countryside flashed past unseen. What the hell was that all about?

Jenny was going to meet me, so I'd best phone her to tell her what had happened.

"Jen, it's me." I told her about the phone call. "You'll still meet me, won't you Jen?"

"Of course I will. I wonder what's happened? Have they caught him at something at last?"

"God knows, they wouldn't say over the phone. You're a love, do you know that? Be there, won't you?"

"Of course."

There was no more sleeping, no more reading either. The buffet trolley passed by and I bought a sandwich and a small bottle of red wine. Yes, red wine. Why not? My guts were turning over like a washing machine on a thousand rev spin cycle. The wine couldn't do me any more damage.

72

Jenny was waiting for me up on the concourse at Penn. The police were nowhere to be seen.

After thanking her for coming, I said "Christ, this is a turn up for the books. I wonder what's happened? Haven't read of any murders in the Village or anything, have you?"

"None that they've announced. Should we wait for the police?"

"No, we'll get trampled under foot here. Let's go. They said that they'd know me."

There were two of them, approaching us from the 8th Avenue exit. One big, beefy man and one smaller, skinnier. They were not in uniform, but they might as well have had NYPD printed on their backs. One millisecond of eye contact was all that was needed.

"Mrs God – Goffrey?" asked the skinnier one.

"Carly Goffrey, yes."

"Sergeant Wilkinson, this is Detective Carter."

"Hi. What's this about?"

"We'll tell you in the car, ma'm."

"In the car? Where are we going?"

"We're going to take you home, ma'm."

∞

The two policemen became noticeably friendlier once we were in the car, a blue Ford Taurus. Jen and I sat in the back.

"Sorry about all this," Sergeant Wilkinson turned in his seat and smiled reassuringly at us as Detective Carter started the engine and pulled out into the rush hour traffic on 8th.

"Is it as a result of my phone call a few weeks ago?"

"How did you know that?"

"Just a guess. But the person I spoke to at the time didn't seem to be interested. Seeing as I hadn't been reported missing in the first place."

"We're always interested, even if at times it seems we're not."

"I thought you'd think I was crazy. Phoning you to tell you I was safe when my husband hadn't even reported me as missing."

"That's what started us thinking. We have a lot of cases, domestics where a spouse runs out, is then reported missing only to turn up safe and well having run home to Mom for the night. But we rarely get them where the, er, victim if you like, phones us up to report that she's safe when we don't know anything about it.

"It was just a routine call log, but it set us thinking. You'd been told you'd been reported missing. But you hadn't been. It just didn't seem right. Was somebody playing a game? So we did a few background checks, just routine you understand."

"And…?"

"You come up clean. But there's something we'd like to check regarding your husband. That's why we called round. There was no reply, so that's why we phoned you – your number was logged when you called us originally. All numbers are."

"What is it? About my husband?"

He pulled a face, obviously reluctant to tell.

"Let's just say," he said, "that we would very much like to get into your apartment. Just to have a little look. With your permission."

And with that, he turned around and was quiet for the rest of the journey.

73

It was dark by the time we pulled up outside the house. I looked up at my apartment windows. They were closed and there were no lights on inside.

"I just want to get some things, then I'm staying around Jenny's tonight," I explained. "How long do you think you'll be?" I opened the car door.

"Hold on, hold on!" Wilkinson reached back and grabbed my arm. "Where do you think you're going?"

"Into my apartment."

"You're not coming up with us."

"But you'll need me to come with you, you'll need me to show you how to get in, there are three locks on the door."

"That's all right, we'll figure it out. You'd be surprised at what we can do."

"Well, be careful of the knives."

"Knives?"

"He likes knives."

"And where exactly are these knives?"

"In the kitchen usually."

"I see. Don't worry, we'll sort it out."

"And what about me and Jenny?"

"You and your friend just wait outside the front door. We'll call you."

"Oh, right, fine. We're to stand out here in the dark on our own. What's to say he's not hiding in the bushes or in the cellar? He knows I've been to the police before - "

"You have?"

"Well… no… It's a long story. He *thinks* I have."

"You and your husband seem to like pretending you have gone to the police."

I said nothing more as we all got out of the car. Dutifully, Jenny and I waited by the front door as the detectives went inside.

It seemed to take forever. Minetta Lane was narrow and tonight the shadows of the night seemed longer. Every rustle, every noise seemed loud and menacing.

We both jumped when my cellphone rang, and I popped out a little circle of air from my bottom. *"We're in the middle of a chain reaction."* A more appropriate ring tone I could not have picked.

"Hello?"

"Right, you can come up Mrs Goffrey. He's not here."

I blew out a sigh and turned to Jenny. "We can go up."

The apartment was as spotless as normal.

The detectives were standing in the living room, two cardboard boxes on the floor in between them. They were the boxes full of CD ROMs that I had previously seen in the bedroom.

"Can you tell us if you think he's gone?" asked the Sergeant. "If you think he's left?"

"I can tell you that straight away. No, he hasn't gone." I pointed. "His computer is still here. He would never go without it."

"Cables," said Detective Carter.

"Sorry, what?"

"Cables, Ma'm. There are no cables coming out of the computer. Just because the machine is still here, doesn't mean he is. He can work on a computer anywhere."

Jenny touched my arm. "Carls, has he gone?"

I bit my lower lip as I looked around. "I don't know…" Slowly, I walked across and entered the bedroom. The bed was unmade, the sheets twisted every way. They seemed to have been quite actively used. At the bottom of the bed was a bowl of candies. Some of his clothes (all black) were still in the wardrobe, but there was something very important missing.

I went back out. "Yes, I think he's gone."

Sergeant Wilkinson raised his eyebrows. "And you are sure how?"

"Teddy's gone."

"Sorry?"

"His teddy bear. He wouldn't go anywhere without his teddy. Even when we went away, he would bring his teddy with us. He must have gone."

Wilkinson looked at me as if I was mad. "Any… er… anything else?"

I shrugged. "Let's look in the kitchen."

Jenny was in there first. "Carly, look at this."

The two policemen crowded into the kitchen behind me.

A bottle of red wine was lying in the precise centre of the kitchen table, a little red bow around its neck.

"He's left you a bottle of wine," Jenny picked it up by the neck, the liquid swirling around inside. "Ouch. Sharp." She was running her finger over the foil top on the mouth of the bottle. She frowned. "It's got a couple of little holes in the top."

"Let me see," Detective Carter took the bottle from her. He nodded and passed it to the other man.

Wilkinson squinted at the cap and then ran his fingers over the foil. Then he stood the bottle on the table and took out a small pocket knife. Deftly he cut around the foil.

"Two little holes," he announced. "Going straight into the cork."

"Strange he would leave you a bottle of red wine, Carly," commented Jenny. "You can't drink red wine."

Wilkinson frowned. "Why can't you drink red wine?"

"The sarcastic bastard knows red wine makes me ill. I'm always ill when I drink it."

"Really…? Well, this cork has got two holes in it. He's probably been drugging you – or even poisoning you."

"What? That's ridiculous. There's always perforations in the foil top of a wine bottle."

"But the perforations don't usually extend down into the cork."

I shook my head. "But if he's going to inject something into it, there's just going to be one hole in it, not two."

"No, if you are going to inject into and through a cork you need two holes. To let the air out and in."

So what did I know?

"But he used to drink it with me."

"Are you sure?"

"Well…" I tried to think back. "I'm sure he did…"

Carter said, "Doesn't mean he's done the same thing previously. There are plenty of ways to drug someone. Maybe this was a one-off special farewell gift for you."

"Christ."

"Has red wine always made you ill?" asked Wilkinson. "When did you start getting ill?"

"Since her marriage," said Jen. "Since she's been with him. She's been in hospital quite a few times."

"Christ." I mumbled again.

"And tell him about the needles, Carls."

"Needles?" Wilkinson raised an eyebrow.

"And… and syringes," I felt sick. "In the bathroom. And scalpels."

"Show me."

I led the way. "And there was a drip bag."

"A what?"

"A drip bag thing that they have in hospitals. He had one of those once."

"What for?"

"Said it was for some research he was doing."

Wilkinson opened the bathroom cabinet. No needles, no syringes, no scalpels, no drip bag. But the Prozac was still there. He picked up the packet. "Yours?"

"No."

"From what I can gather, and from what we know- "

"What do you know?"

" – your husband is not the depressive sort." He looked at the label. "These would need to be prescribed. Have you got his doctor's number?"

"It will be in the phone."

"Same doctor as you?"

"No, he kept the one he had when he was living in TriBeCa."

Wilkinson had picked up the phone. "How do you work this...? Oh, I see." He scrolled down the phone memory. "Doctor, Gary. Reckon that's it, yes? Mind if I call him?"

"Go ahead."

He pressed the dial key and waited with the phone to his ear. Then he pressed the red key, found redial and put the phone back to his ear again. He smiled. "Number unobtainable. Now how did I know that was going to happen? You don't know the doctor's name, have his address or anything?"

"No, no I don't."

"O...kay."

"Sergeant," Carter was calling from the living room. "Have you seen this?" He was holding an envelope in his hand, one of the handful of letters I had picked up from downstairs on my way in. "From *Liberty Travel*."

Wilkinson took it. "It's addressed to him. May I open it?"

I nodded.

Once again, he took out his pocket knife and slid it carefully across the top of the flap. He pulled out the single sheet and studied it. "It's a receipt for a one-way ticket to Sydney, Australia, via Los Angeles. Leaving on twenty-sixth." He looked at his watch. "Two days ago. Paid in cash. Ticket to be collected at JFK."

"Then he's gone!" Jenny clapped her hands together as I sat down on the couch.

"Probably. But not necessarily," said Wilkinson.

I looked up from between my fingers. "What do you mean?"

"He might not have got on the flight. This might be a red herring, to put us off the scent."

"Do those things actually happen outside of movies and books?"

"No, probably not in this situation. But you would be surprised. We can make enquiries. We can find out whether he took the flight."

"Thank you. Thank you for everything."

"Just one thing, though," said Carter. "His keys."

"What?"

"Usually in a domestic, the leaving party leaves their keys. Thrown at the other person, or across the room or through the letter box. We don't have his keys, do we?"

I shook my head. "No, we don't."

"Then I suggest you change the locks," advised Wilkinson. "Just in case. And you might not want to stay here tonight."

"I wasn't going to."

Carter bent over and stacked the two boxes on top of each other. Then, bending at the knees, he picked them up.

"You're taking those?"

"With your permission."

"Of course, of course."

"If you need us, call us." Wilkinson gave me his card. I took it as I stood up.

Wilkinson paused, as if he was wondering whether to say anything else. "Mrs Goffrey, with what you've told us and with what we know, I must tell you that I think your husband is a very dangerous man."

The hairs on my arms were standing on end. "What are you

saying?"

"I can't tell you more at this time, but just be thankful he wasn't here tonight. I honestly do believe he has gone. And if past form is anything to go by - "

"Past form?"

" – you'll never hear from him again. Try to put this all behind you. Get on with your life. Talk to a counselor if you need to." He took one of the boxes from Carter. "But above all - "

"Yes?"

"Be careful, Mrs Goffrey."

With that, they left.

Feel my hate

Georgie sat in the left window seat in the back row of the Boeing 777 as it headed south. They were one hour out of Sydney.

Two days this journey had taken them. Two days!

Thank God Daddy had been in a good mood for most of the time. A night's stopover in Bangkok had helped. Georgie had been left in the hotel room while Daddy went out and enjoyed something he called 'The Fleshpots'.

Georgie was used to sitting with his knees under his chin, but now he was getting tired of sitting in that position in a plane. His bottom was numb.

It is all your fault, Mommy. You have driven us out of our home. You have made us run away. You have made us leave the country. And we had all been getting on so well. What was wrong, Mommy? Couldn't you take a joke?

I hate you, Mommy.

I wish you were dead, Mommy.

But it's not over yet.

You still had to pay, Mommy

74

I couldn't wait to get out of the place.

What did they mean, Gary was dangerous? I know I'd said it before, but that was just me from my domestic perspective. When the police said 'dangerous' it took on a whole new meaning. What was it they knew? What was it they weren't telling me? I knew Gary was weird, that he liked playing his little games, but this sounded much more serious... Much more sinister.

I spent a fitful night at Helena's. I was restive and I felt sure I was setting myself up for some more crazy nightmares, but none came. I can't remember dreaming of anything.

The next morning, Helena gave me her *Yellow Pages*.

I knew there was a Paragon Locksmith up near MAC in Christopher Street. The guy who answered must have thought it was his birthday. Did he hear right? I needed the apartment locks changed (times three), and the main front door locks changed. For the front door I needed nineteen (yes, that's right, nineteen) sets of keys (two for me, a set for each of the three agents and the rest for the other occupants of the building). Yes, he took credit cards.

I telephoned all three agents to let them know what I was doing, and why. The keys were being cut today, the locks were being changed tomorrow. Could they come round tomorrow and pick up their new keys?

Two were quite amenable but one, Simon, our agent and agent for the apartment on the ground floor where two gay boys had lived until recently, was prickly. He said it would be a bit inconvenient for him to come round, could I drop the keys off to him? His office was only up the road.

That, I said, was the exact reason why he should have no problem coming around, being so close. I was very busy arranging all this and I didn't have time to be a delivery service as well. (Okay, I was a cow. Changing the locks was all my fault anyway. But I was not in the mood.) With a sigh, Simon said he'd see what he could do.

Come the next morning, there was me, Jenny and Helena handing out keys to all and sundry, knocking on doors or waylaying people as they went off to work, and of course each time we had to give the explanation. By nine in the morning we were exhausted.

We adjourned to my apartment, where coffee awaited.

As we took a few moments of quietness, I looked around the place from my position on the couch. There were still books here on the shelves, still things in the kitchen and the bathroom. The place still looked lived in. But, if the police were right, Gary had gone for good. This apartment was therefore in a state of interregnum: one occupant gone, the other deciding whether or not to depart. When we had first moved in, the place had seemed welcoming. Then over the years it had filled me with foreboding every time I came back to it. Towards the end, it had filled me with fear. And now? Now it seemed just sad.

The doorbell jolted me out of my reverie.

The three of us looked over at the entryphone. The locksmith perhaps? If so, he was early. I had asked him to come in the afternoon, after I had made sure I had caught everybody and had given out the new keys before the front door lock was changed.

I went over. "Hello?"

"Hello Carly, it's Simon."

"Who?"

"*Simon*. You insisted I came round? Can you let me in?"

"The locks haven't been changed yet, you've still got the key."

"Just let me in."

"Whatever." I pressed the door release.

I had never actually met Simon, although he was an acquaintance of Gary's and it was through him we had gotten this apartment, but Gary had told me he was as gay as Carlos and Michael, the two boys who had recently moved out of the apartment downstairs. And that was gay with a capital G-A-Y.

Footsteps on the stairs outside, and then a knock on my door. I picked up the new keys ready to give to him, but he barged straight in when I opened the door.

"God, you look busy," he blurted. "Anything going on?"

I frowned. He knew what was 'going on', I had explained it to him on the phone. That was why I needed to change the locks. "I'm just having a bit of a tidy up, post husband and all that."

"The place is a mess."

"Thank you very much." But he was right.

"Everything all right then is it, Carly?" He was nervy, chatty.

That was twice now he had used my name. Worrying. Because I didn't think I had ever told him it. When I rang him up I said it was "The girl who lives upstairs Minetta Lane." But he did look vaguely familiar. Perhaps we *had* met at some time, at a Do or something.

I passed him the new keys.

"Ah, yes, thanks. I've got some builders coming today, to start work on the apartment downstairs before I re-let it. If you're going to be here, I hope it won't be too noisy. Talking of keys..." He fumbled in his jacket pocket and produced three keys on a ring. "Don't know whose these are, do you?"

I looked at them in his palm. "No, how should I know?"

"Well, you've got three locks and everything on your door. I came across these downstairs the other day, in the empty apartment. Not yours then?"

Detective Carter's words of two days ago repeated in my head. *"Usually in a domestic, the leaving party leaves their keys. Thrown at the other person, or across the room or through the letter box. We don't have his keys, do we?"*

I couldn't tell whether or not these were Gary's keys. All the apartments had the same three lock combinations on their front doors. His skull key fob was not attached. And I did not, under any circumstances, want to try them in the apartment locks. If they were his, how on earth did they get into the empty apartment?

"No," I said, "not mine."

"Oh well, I just thought you might know. Thanks for the new ones. I'd better go down and see if those big strong boys have arrived yet."

It was as Simon turned and left that realisation hit me.

As he thumped down the stairs, my anus trembled like San Francisco in 1906.

"Good God, Carly!" laughed Jenny. "He must have heard that!"

I tried to laugh, to make light of it, as I hobbled to the bathroom with my thighs pressed tight together, butt cheeks clenched. Helena and Jenny didn't know, but I had literally shit myself. The shock had slammed through my stomach more effectively that a too hot colonic irrigation.

As I sat on the toilet and began the awful task of cleaning myself up, my right hand began to shake. What the hell was going on?

Simon had known my name, yet I was sure I had never told him. Simon had acted familiarly, yet I was sure I had never met him. Simon had keys (whether or not found in the apartment downstairs) that could have been Gary's, and he had attempted to give them back to me.

And as I caught his sideways profile as he had left, I had recognised him.

I had met him before.

Simon was one of the two men who had been having sex with Gary in my nightmares.

75

Have you ever tried to flush your panties down the toilet? Wrong move, I can tell you. But what was I to do? I could hardly carry my soiled (and then some) underwear back out in my hands, and I couldn't ask my friends to look the other way while a pair of pooey drawers came through.

It took three attempts, the toilet water and its contents coming right up to the top edge of the bowl, but they finally went down. I stood there after the third flush, staring down into the bowl, praying they would not sneakily reappear. They did not. Success! I just hope I hadn't blocked up the entire house somewhere in the mysterious labyrinth that was plumbing. Or the whole block. Or the whole neighbourhood.

I could see the headlines:

SOILED UNDERWEAR CAUSES MASSIVE NEW YORK BLOW-BACK
Mystery woman sought
'She needs urgent medical attention' say police

So it was a pantie-less Carly that took her two friends to lunch at the café down on 6th Avenue. My friends were unaware of my commando-like attire, and I did not enlighten them.

The Golden Horn was a Turkish-owned kebab, burger-type place, and it served the needs of the local residents well. In the early years of our marriage, Gary and I used to visit here often - but in the last months he had refused to come down here. He gave some excuse about it being too greasy.

Because we were expecting the locksmith in the afternoon, we had come down early. There was only one other customer in the place, a grizzled old man who looked Turkish himself, sitting with a pot of coffee in one corner.

We had just sat down at a table when the door of the place opened again. And in walked Simon.

He couldn't help but see us. "Hi Carly. Ladies." He nodded awkwardly.

"Hello."

He sat down two tables away from us.

The waitress came, took our orders (grease burgers and fries for three), took Simon's, and went back through the mysterious Staff Only doors. Soon we heard the sound of sizzling from out back.

We spoke about girly things until our food was served. Two tables away, Simon just sat there. Was he trying to listen to us?

He had just a coffee, so we were only two mouthfuls into our grease burgers when he got up and left.

"Strange," said Jenny as we watched him go. "What was that about? It was like he was checking on us."

"You think?" said Helena. "Perhaps he just wanted a coffee. He's waiting for the builders, isn't he?"

"Nothing would surprise me any more," I sighed. "I think I'm in Weirdsville, Ohio, Population Two with one of them missing."

"No, no, you're thinking of Hitler's underpants, dear." Hels just about got it out before we all erupted with laughter.

When we had calmed down, I caught the waitress's eye and gave the universal mime for the check.

"Do you know that guy who was in here?" I asked her as I

counted out the money.

"Him? Yeh. Used to come in here a lot."

"Not recently?"

"No, that's the first time I've seen him since he came back."

"Came back?"

"You hear everything in my job. He's been away. In Australia."

My purse thudded as it hit the table top. Quickly I picked it up.

"Australia?"

"He's been there for a few months. Buying property or something."

"Does he always come in on his own?"

"No, I've never seen him on his own before. Usually he's with his boy friends."

"Thanks, you've been a honey." I added a fifty per cent tip and gave her the money.

"Thank *you*."

I raised my eyebrows at Jenny and Helena.

"Population Three maybe…?" I suggested.

76

With the locks changed, I was tempted to stay the night in the apartment – but with Weird Simon around I decided one more night away might be the more prudent option.

Helena put me up again but she had family things to do the next day, so Jenny picked me up just after 09:00.

Just after 09:01, and before I had even fastened my seat belt, my cellphone rang.

"Hello Carly, it's Roger."

"Roger?"

"Sergeant Wilkinson."

"Oh hi, Ser – Roger." I made a face to Jenny.

"Just to let you know, we're sending some of our CSU guys round this morning. They just want to have a little look at a few things."

"CSU!"

"Nothing to worry about. You are at the apartment, aren't you?"

"No, but I'm on my way."

"Okay, fine. They won't be there long and they'll try not to get in your way. But if you're not at the apartment, would you mind not going in yet? Less contamination."

"I'll wait outside for them."

"Apparently," I explained to Jenny as we pulled out into the traffic, "the police are still interested. CSU are coming round. I wish they would damn well tell me what's going on."

We arrived in Minetta Lane just before 10:00 and parked behind a white transit van. There were three men outside the front of the house: Simon standing over two men who were hard at work.

I got out of the car, cigarette in my hand. The side door of the van was open, and there were workmen-like tools inside. Painted on the door in red letters was **Is**. On the body of the van underneath was **uilders**.

"*Isis Builders*," explained Jenny. "It's on the back as well. Strange name. The goddess of justice, amongst other things – but these morons probably don't know that."

"It's *Sisi* backwards," I threw my cigarette butt on the floor and stood on it. "That's more up their alley!"

Simon saw my action. "If you don't mind!" he said tetchily. "I'm just cleaning this place up. We've water-jetted all this this morning, so I'd rather it wasn't dirtied again straightaway."

"Sorry, sorry." I kicked the butt out onto the road.

"Now we're re-cementing this bit, as you can see," continued Simon. "So please be careful"

"We will."

He saw we were making no move to go inside. "Are you waiting for somebody?"

"Yeh."

"Who?"

"None of your business."

Bridling, he turned and went up the stairs into the house.

At that moment another smaller van pulled up behind Jenny's car. Quite a little convoy was building.

I expected them to be in the white overalls you see at crime scenes on TV, but the two men who emerged from the van wore smart-casual clothes. One carried a little briefcase.

"Mrs - ?" said the taller of the two.

"Carly, yes. You're from, er, Mr Wilkinson?"

"That's right. This is Dick, I'm Harry." (I didn't say it. I wanted to, but I didn't.) "Can you show us up to your apartment?"

Dick, the smaller one was looking at the ground. "Hm." He tipped the toe of his shoe, marking the newly-laid cement. "Fresh. Hasn't gone off yet."

"No," I explained, "one of the agents has the builders in. They've just done that. They're inside. Actually," I lowered my voice, "before you go up to the apartment... There's a cellar downstairs. I'd like to see if there's anything down there."

"Why should there be anything down there?" asked Harry.

I thought of the times Gary used to take the rubbish out and be gone for ten minutes or more. I thought of the grazes on his knee. I thought, irrationally, that perhaps he was hiding down there, waiting to kill me.

"I don't know." I tried to be girly. "Just in case my husband has left anything down there. I'm too scared to go myself."

Dick softened. "How do we get down?"

"There's stairs at the side." I pointed to the left.

"We'll have a look for you."

While they were gone, I was thinking of the only time I had been down in that cellar: when we had first arrived at the house, I had gone down to check the place out. It was dark and dingy; there had been a couple of old pictures in frames and an old wooden chair. The walls were unplastered and there was soil for a floor, no concrete.

They were back up again within three minutes. From where we were standing out front we could see the two officers coming back up the stairs at the side. At the same time, Simon flounced out of the front door.

Simon pointed to the ground from the top of the stairs. "Who's damn well trodden in my cement?"

"We did," said Harry as they came round the corner.

"And who the hell are you?"

"Who the hell are you, sir?"

The change in Simon was tangible. "Ah. Sorry, but I've just had this laid."

"I'm sure they can smooth it over, sir."

"Yes. Yes, I'm sure they can." With a movement just the right side of haste, Simon went back inside.

Up in the apartment, I handed over the bottle of red wine with the holes in the cork. Then the officers conducted a thorough search of the place, pulling out all drawers, feeling behind them, occasionally bagging a stray computer disk, flicking through books. In the kitchen, they bagged the knives.

In all, the search took them an hour. At the end they had a small bag of Gary's remaining computer disks, an even smaller bag containing the knives and a few needles, syringes and scalpels, which they had found in the desk not in the bathroom, and a big rubbish sack containing the clothes Gary had left behind. Dick carried the computer under his arm ("It's probably been wiped clean, but we'll check.")

To their credit, they put everything back neat and tidy. Had I not been with them, I wouldn't have known they had been there.

"So what now?" I asked as they were leaving.

"That's our job done," said Harry. "Sergeant Wilkinson will probably be in touch."

"Oh, okay."

Jenny didn't want to leave me on my own in the place, but I had resolved that I would stay there. This was my apartment, dammit. After spending another hour with me over two strong coffees, Jenny left.

I was there as I wanted to be. Alone.

It felt strange, but also it felt different. Good different. The police had effectively removed every trace of Gary. All his clothes were gone, those damn needles, syringes and scalpels, even the nasty bottle of wine he had left me. All that was left of him were most of his books, piled on top of each other in a corner of the living room, a few odd papers that the police weren't interested in, and a computer monitor without wires.

Was I at last free of him?

77

My night's sleep was not as good as I had hoped it would be. I had no nightmares, but I woke at every little sound, every little creak of the house. Was this him? Was he in the room? Was he coming to get me?

No, he wasn't. Chances were that he was back in Australia by now. But somehow I had the feeling that, even if he was truly gone, his tentacles were still stretching across the world, interfering with my life, threatening me.

The last thing I needed was a damn phone call.

I had a jar of *Nescafé* in my hand when the phone shrilled out from the living room. The coffee granules shot across the work surface in the kitchen, about twenty cups-worth. Christ, I was jumpy today.

The phone was incessant. I thought about ignoring it, but it could be one of my friends, or even the police.

"Hello?"

There was a pause for recognition, then a male voice said "Oh Carly, what are you doing in the apartment?" The voice had a strong German accent.

"Gustaf?" It was a friend of Gary's, another photographer of course.

"Hello."

"What do you mean what am I doing in the apartment? I live in the apartment, don't I?"

"*Jah. Jah.* It's just that you're not normally there."

"You're right, I'm normally out working. One of us has to. But I'm having to spend a bit of time at home at the moment."

"Ah."

"You obviously haven't phoned up to speak to me. Did you want Gary?"

"Is he there?"

"No."

"Do you know when he will be back?"

"No."

"Do you know where I can find him?"

"How about in hell?"

"Zorry?"

"Did he put you up to this, Gustaf? Do you think I'm stupid? How many times do you or any of his other friends call this landline? You always call his cell."

"Yess, but he iss not - "

"I don't care what he is not. Just piss off, will you. And don't ring this number again."

I slammed down the phone. Two seconds later, my cell started ringing. The cheeky bastard!

I picked it up from the coffee table. *Number Withheld.*

I pressed the green key. "Look I fucking don't know where he is, I don't care where he is, he is no longer part of my life - !"

"Carly?"

The female voice stopped me in mid rant.

"T- Tara?" It was the manager of MAC in Christopher Street.

"You okay?"

"Yes – Yes! Sorry, I thought it was somebody else."

"How you doing?"

"Oh not bad, you know. It feels strange, I can't believe he's really gone."

"I've got a letter here for you."

"A letter?"

"Sent to the shop, addressed to you. Shall I send it round?"

"No. No, I'll come and get it. A trip out will do me good. Don't know who it's from, do you?"

"No, there's no return address."

"Okay, I'll come by later. Fancy lunch?"

"That would be nice. You can tell me everything that's been happening."

"Oh God, how long have you got? I said lunch, not the rest of your life."

I recognised the writing on the envelope immediately. It was Gary's. Why the hell would he be writing me a letter? And why would he send it to MAC and not to the apartment? Unless he thought I was never going back to there.

Tara must have sensed my tension when I looked at the envelope, but I stuffed it into my bag unopened. That was a job for later, when I was on my own.

Lunch with Tara was nice, but I was anxious to get home. In fact, I couldn't wait to get home - I ripped open the letter as I walked down 6th Avenue.

Carly,

As of 29 April I will be vacating the apartment. Move back in if you wish.

Regards,

Gary

I should have been pleased. I was pleased. But, as always with Gary, I was also puzzled. *As of 29 April.* Why the twenty-ninth? The letter was postmarked the twenty-sixth, the same day as he supposedly flew back to Australia. Why the three days difference?

I reflected ruefully that it was just as well for his sake that he hadn't been there for those three days, what with all the police activity that had been going on.

So was this it? Closure? Could I now pick up the sticks of my life? Could I be normal again?

Most of the stuff he had left behind had been taken by the police, but there was still the pile of books and a few old papers.

A quick phone call to Jacqui and she agreed to come round that evening and help me clear this man out of my apartment, out of my life, forever.

78

Gary always wrote his name in his books. Sometimes he would write both our names. I hadn't really been interested at the time, but now I wanted to see exactly which books he regarded as 'ours'. After a bagel and two cigarettes, and armed with a litre bottle of wine, Jac and I set about putting the books in piles. Those with his name only in one pile, those with both our names in another pile. A quick and easy job.

With one hitch.

Always, always a hitch. Gary might be on the other side of the world by now, but his influence, his Little Ways still lingered like a guest that had overstayed his welcome.

Because after we had finished sorting the books, we didn't just have two piles – we had three. A 'Gary' pile, a 'Gary and Carly' pile – and a 'Carly' pile.

There were two books in which he had written just my name. Books I wasn't even aware of. One was about cats: a sick book by a Japanese photographer showing how you can play with cats, make them jump, make them stretch, make them dangle. There were pictures which would have been considered cruel in the West.

The other book was *Memnoch The Devil* by Anne Rice.

Why had he left me that? I remembered him wanting me to

watch *Interview With The Vampire* one night, but I hadn't liked it and had gone to bed. Anne Rice had written that also, of course. Was this his little way of provoking my memories?

We piled all the books into three bin sacks. Some of the books I had seen before, some I wasn't even aware he had. There was the autobiography of Gary Glitter, the English pop star pedophile. One about photographers in South America who like redressing dead bodies and putting them in positions. One by Jock Sturgess who was arrested by the CIA for photographing young children, which started the ensuing debate: is it art or is it pedophilia?

Interesting. These 'dodgy' books had both our names in, whereas all the books that could be regarded as normal had just his name in.

Well, my name, his name, our names, Memnoch the Devil's name, I didn't care – they were out of the apartment as of now. I couldn't give these things to charity, so they would go in the bin.

Jacqui helped me carry them downstairs. I was praying that none of the other residents would come out as we were carrying them down. People liked books, and their natural reaction would be "Are you throwing those away? Can I have a look, see if there's anything of interest?"

Thankfully nobody came out, but the thought stayed with me as we carried the sacks over to the wheelie bin. It was four days until the bin men came, anyone could find the books in that time. I said as much to Jac.

"I've got an idea," I continued, nodding to the stairway at the side of the house. "Let's store these in the cellar. No one will go down there in the next three days. We'll bring them back up the night before the bins are emptied."

"You sure?" Jacqui was wary. "You said you'd only been down there once and it gave you the creeps."

"That was three years ago. The police checked the place out the other day, there's nothing there. We can't leave the books here in case anyone finds them – and I don't want the damn things in the apartment."

She nodded in understanding. "Okay, let's do it."

The gate creaked as we pushed it open. I led the way down the small stairway. I half expected the door to be locked, but it wasn't. (Had it ever been?) I expected the door to be stiff, and I gave it a hard kick. It slammed open, the bang echoing off the emptiness inside. The musty smell of earth and stale air wafted out.

The evening light was not enough to see by, so I fumbled for the light switch on the wall, Jac right behind me.

I know, you're thinking that I flicked the switch up and down frantically but the light didn't go on. Sorry to disappoint, but I flicked the switch once and a fluorescent in the middle of the ceiling flashed into life. We both stepped inside.

I think it was at that moment that I finally went insane.

Behind and to the right of me, Jacqui exclaimed "Oh fucking hell, what's that?"

I just stared. The open top of the sack I was carrying flopped forward, and the books began to fall out one by one.

And then I screamed, and I screamed, and I screamed…

79

"They weren't there when CSU looked the other day." Sergeant Roger Wilkinson sat on the couch in my apartment cradling a mug of coffee in his hands and looking at the objects which we had found in the cellar.

He had been reluctant to come round when Jacqui had phoned him, but once we had told him what we had found he had agreed to come take a look. Neither Jacqui nor I had touched the things, but with the help of my cooking tongs Wilkinson had picked two of them up and put them into a brown supermarket sack and then brought them up to the apartment. He had left the dirty duvet, the pillow and the empty chip bags and chocolate wrappers down there.

Now the items were tipped out again in the center of my living room. As you can imagine, I was none too happy.

The three of us stared at the two objects. One was a child's orange padded parka coat; it was old and dirty and looked like it had been hidden away somewhere for years, perhaps even buried.

The other object was a drawing. It looked something like The Three Pigs. The pig in the middle had been crudely colored in, all black. The two smaller pigs on either side were colored orange. The outline of the pigs was pre-drawn, but the coloring was rough, done in crayon, with hardly any attempt to keep within the shapes of the pigs. The sort of coloring-in a child would do. Under one of the pigs the word TOM had been written in a shaky hand. Between the other two pigs the same hand had written the letter G.

"Interesting colors," I said.

"Interesting?" asked Wilkinson.

"The orange pigs – they match the coat. And the big black pig in the middle? Gary never wore anything but black."

"I see."

"I think maybe it's time you or somebody wrote down my whole story. Took a statement from me or something."

"But how did they get down there? The place was clean the other day."

"Maybe he's still around." It didn't sound as nervous as I felt.

"Oh no, he 's not." Wilkinson smiled. "I was going to ring you tomorrow. We've had it confirmed by Australian Immigration. He arrived at Sydney on April 30th. He hasn't left again, he's still there. Staying with his mother. He's being covertly watched."

"Then how *did* these things get down there?"

He shrugged. "Maybe he still has… friends. Maybe someone close to him put them down there. Or someone else in the block?"

"But why?"

He finished his coffee and put his mug on the table. "To keep them safe and away from prying eyes." He looked up. "Perhaps until the bin men came. No one would think of going down there."

What had he just said? What was he implying?

"You bastard," said Jacqui.

I couldn't believe what I had just heard. "Are you insinuating that I put them down there?"

"I'm not insinuating anything, Carly. But they got down there somehow, they didn't just materialise. And it was your idea to put the books down there until the bin men come."

"I think you should leave now," I said. "And take those fucking things with you. Have your CSU boys look *them* over."

"Sure." He was picking the things up again with the tongs and putting them back in the sack. "I didn't mean to offend." He stood up. As he walked to the front door, he said "What you have to appreciate is that your husband *has* gone. And believe me, what we know of his past, he won't be coming back. He's out of our jurisdiction – indeed, even if he was here what could we charge him with? It's not an offence to keep a small coat or eat potato chips or chocolate."

"How about drugging his wife?"

He looked me in the eyes. "To what end? Did he kill you? No. Do we have any actual proof he drugged you? No."

"Test me."

"What?"

"Test me. Surely there's something you can do to see if there's drugs in my system."

"Of course there is, but - "

"But nothing. Test me. Or I'll take this higher."

He looked at me, as if weighing up the possibilities. "You want us to test you?"

"Yes. And if it's proved that he has been drugging me, then you can extradite him or something, surely?"

"Or at least get him if he ever comes back to the USA," said Jacqui.

Was that amusement in Wilkinson's eyes? "Okay," he said, "if you want us to test you, we'll test you. You free tomorrow?"

I was taken aback. "Er... Yes."

"I'll come for you at ten."

80

Spot on, Wilkinson was waiting outside at 10:00 in the Ford Taurus. He frowned when he saw Jenny coming out of the house with me.

"I've asked Jenny to come with me," I explained as we climbed into the back of the car. "Don't mind, do you?"

"No, no."

"Where are we going? The station house?"

"Contrary to popular belief, we don't have doctors permanently assigned to us. Some local doctors take it in turns to be on call. I'm taking you to Doctor Wang's surgery."

Doctor Wang's surgery was on the first floor of an old building on West 12th Street by Greenwich Street . We parked around on Jane Street, and Wilkinson accompanied us down an alley and through a back door. We entered a small, bare room with a couple of chairs and some old magazines on a decrepit wooden table. Discourteously, I wondered what other activities Doctor Wang got up to to warrant a 'back door' waiting room. It wouldn't be hard to guess.

"His morning surgery finished at ten, so he shouldn't be too long. I'll go tell him you're here." Wilkinson disappeared through another door, closing it behind him.

Jenny and I looked at each other. "Medicare?" I smiled.

"Not even," said Jenny. "More like some of the National Health Service places we have in England."

"Still, taxpayers' money and all that."

"Are you sure you want to go through with this, Carly?"

I had no doubt. "Oh yes."

Wilkinson popped his head back round the door. "Carly, could you come this way?"

We both got up.

"Only Carly," said Wilkinson. "You wait here please, Jenny."

Reluctantly, my friend sat back down.

Along a small, narrow corridor and into another room. This one was also small, but it contained an examination table, a chair and a cabinet that held God knows what. On top of the cabinet was a steel tray, covered with a towel.

A Chinese man was waiting by the examination table.

"Good morning," he was polite but perfunctory.

I nodded.

"Please, if you would sit down," he tapped the edge of the table. "I would like to ask you some questions first and then I will examine you. Then I will ask you some more questions."

"Okay."

I heard the door close. Sergeant Wilkinson was standing with his back against it.

The doctor's questions were the usual: age, weight, height etc. Any children? No chance.

"All right. Now I will examine you. Canyupee?"

"I'm sorry?"

"Pee. Can you pee?" He held up a specimen jar.

"Oh! Er, yes, I think so. Here?"

"There is a toilet next door if you would prefer."

Considering there were no modesty curtains in this room, I certainly did prefer.

When I returned with an inch in the bottom of the jar, there was a woman in the room along with the doctor and the police officer. I passed the warm container to the doctor, who cupped it in his hand and swirled my pee around as if it was fine brandy, then held it up to the light. "This is my nurse," he explained as he put the specimen jar down on the cabinet. "For propriety."

I nodded. She was not dressed as a nurse, she was in jeans and a white shirt. And she looked very young – or was it me that was getting old? Whatever, I was glad she was there. I had expected Sergeant Wilkinson to leave the room, but he remained in his position guarding the door.

"Right," said Doctor Wang. "Could you get undressed please?"

I hesitated. I had always been one for laughing at modesty screens in doctor's surgeries. What was the point, I used to ask, of getting dressed and undressed behind screens when the doctor would be seeing you naked and touching your most intimate parts? But now it was payback time – I dearly wished we had screens here.

But we didn't. I closed my mind to the three other people in the room and began to unbutton my top.

"Take off everything please," said Doctor Wang. He stood away from me, probably for propriety's sake like he said, but it only made me feel as if I was performing. A separate, intimate entertainment for an audience of three. A private dance.

I had lost a lot of weight, and I didn't feel good about myself, so I consoled myself with the fact that this would be the least sexy striptease that any of them had ever seen. No guns in your pockets today boys.

I didn't look at them as I stood there completely naked.

"Sit on the table," Doctor Wang was putting on surgical gloves. He whipped the towel off the tray on the side to reveal an array of surgical instruments, including a speculum.

He examined my hands, my nails, my feet, my hair, my eyes, my tongue. He took a swab from my mouth, and I knew what was coming next.

At least I thought I did.

He was going to ask me to lie down, knees up, legs apart.

But he didn't.

Instead, he said "Would you kneel on all fours on the table please."

I was shocked. "I'm sorry?"

"Kneel on the table please."

"Why on earth should I?"

"I know what I am doing."

"But - "

The doctor sighed. "I am required to take vaginal and rectal swabs. In my experience this is the easiest way."

I have never, ever, felt so humiliated or so exposed. I hoped Wilkinson was doing the decent thing and not looking. About the nurse, I did not care. With the two fingers of his left hand, the doctor prised my butt cheeks apart and inserted what he had to insert. I felt just a light tickle.

I heard a *clink* in the tray, and then my lips were opened in a similar fashion.

Another *clink*.

"Right, please sit back down again." The doctor turned to Wilkinson who, to his credit, did not seem to have been looking at me. He was a bit flushed though. "This is for drugs, yes?"

Wilkinson nodded.

"Then I will need some hair samples as well. If you don't mind, ma'm?" He picked up some scissors.

I shrugged. Why should I mind? You've just been probing my arse, you've got a glassful of my pee, you've had your fingers up my pussy - do you think I mind if you take a few hairs as well?

He took twelve tiny samples from twelve different places on my head, putting each one carefully into a separate sealable plastic bag, which he then labelled.

"Stand up please."

This I had expected. Twelve small samples of my pubes. Perhaps I should have asked for a Brazilian while he was down there?

Then, thank God, it was over. "Okay, get dressed please."

The whole room seemed to relax. I never knew what a great sense of security it would give me just to put my panties back on. My ass itched where he had been up there, but I resisted the urge to insert a finger and scratch like a maniac.

More questions as I dressed, the first one a shocker. Conversationally, Doctor Wang asked "If your husband was to walk in here right now, how would you feel?"

I stopped, hands behind my back, doing up my bra. I just hoped this wasn't some macabre *This Is Your Life*. "How would I feel? Petrified."

"And on a scale of zero to ten, how would you describe sex with your husband?"

I thought carefully before answering. As I pulled up my jeans, I said "O for Obligatory."

Doctor Wang looked at me. "Interesting word."

"Isn't it?" I smiled insincerely. "Is that it?"

"Yes. Thank you."

"What now?" I asked Wilkinson. "Do you want to take me to the station and take a statement from me or something?"

He shook his head. He seemed as relieved as I was that it was all over. "That won't be necessary. We now just wait for the results of the tests. But to save us the time, you could tell us what other extra-curricular drugs might be in your system. This is a two year cycle we're looking at."

"Two years?"

"That's how long the traces remain. Is there anything?"

"Well, I'm not an habitual user or anything but... two years?... you might find traces of pot and cocaine."

"Okay," Wilkinson nodded to the doctor.

"What exactly will you be looking for?" I asked.

"Rohypnol, GHB, that sort of thing."

"GBH?"

"GHB."

The doctor explained. "Gammahydroxybuterate. Liquid ecstasy."

"Liquid ecstasy?"

"One of the side effects," explained Wilkinson, "is memory loss."

The doctor and nurse went one way down the corridor, the policeman and I walked back the way we'd came.

"How long till the results come through?" I asked.

"Usually take about four months."

"Four months!"

"Resources are limited. And your case is not exactly urgent."

"Oh it isn't, is it?"

"Carly, your husband has gone. We know he is in Australia. Can't you understand that? He's not coming back."

We reached the outer room where Jenny was sitting patiently.

"Can I give you a lift back?" asked Wilkinson.

Jenny could see my grumpy face. "No," I said, "no thanks. We'll walk."

"Okay then," he nodded. "We'll be in touch."

We watched his back departing and then we left ourselves, walking past his car and out onto West 4th Street.

"How was it?" asked Jenny.

"Awful," I said, my voice low. "I feel like I've just starred in a porno movie."

"Fancy a coffee, something to eat?"

"Right now, I fancy like a long hot shower – with the biggest and roughest loufer I can get my hands on."

PART EIGHT

Revelations

81

Three days later, I died.

I had been expecting something, so when it came it was, in a perverse way, a relief. But it was the shock of it, the nature of it, that I had not been expecting.

My descent into madness had taken the full three years I was with Gary. Even now I feel rigid with frustration when I think of the times I tried to describe him to people, and they would nod in fake understanding, humoring me, asking me if I could be exaggerating or imagining things. But my death happened when I was all alone. Gary was thousands of miles away across the other side of the world, and yet he was as responsible for my death as if he had gotten hold of one of his beloved knives and plunged it into me.

What am I talking about? Has this suddenly become a paranormal tale written by a dead woman? No, it hasn't. As I write this, I am still living. But I am not as I was. It was a mundane object that finally killed any vestige of the old Carly.

I was spooked on my own in the apartment, and maybe I was indeed letting my imagination run away with me. How many times did I tell myself that Gary wasn't in the country? He had gone, the police had confirmed it. That creak over there was just the floorboards, not him coming to get me. That bump as I was getting into bed was just somebody in one of the other apartments.

Although the apartment felt different now that his malign presence was no longer around, I was still restive. I just *knew* that something was going to happen – and I was right.

Gary Goffrey had used many devices to scare me, to intimidate me, to play those mind games with me. At that time I did not know he had used other people as well, but I was soon to find out. But this time he used the one person whom I thought would never, ever, be used against me. It was the ultimate triumph for him.

He used *me*.

I was twitchy, couldn't sleep. For a while now, I had been thinking about sorting out my collection of purses and bags – I had far too many. A lot of them were freebies, Shoot Loot, so I thought I would sort out those I hadn't used for a while, if at all, and give them to my friends, a way of thanking them for being there for me. (The bags were all designer gear. While Shoot Loot is no match for Academy Awards Goodie Bags, us make-up girls do all right thank you.)

I sat in the living room, television on low (the early hours *CNN News* reporting that yet another Senator had been caught with his dick where it shouldn't be). The coffee table lamp gave me enough light to see by. I had sorted out ten bags in all, and I was feeling pretty pleased as I imagined giving them to my friends.

I would wrap them up nicely, and I made a mental note to get some wrapping paper tomorrow.

Most of the bags still had the filling paper inside them, but as I was lining them up on the floor next to the couch, one of them *bumped* – that little knock you sometimes get when you buy a CD or DVD that is loose within its case.

I frowned. It was the Armani bag that I had singled out for

Jacqui.

I picked it up and, as we humans do, shook it again. *Bump.*

There was something in there. Probably an accessory for the bag that I hadn't noticed previously, a key ring or pocket book or something. Well, that's a bonus for you, Jac.

I opened the bag and peered inside.

And I froze.

Slowly I put my hand in and brought out the object inside.

It was a computer disk.

It was a copy or a home-made disk, for there was no proprietary printing on it. There was just a number. 27.

It was the disk I had seen on top of the box of disks in the bedroom when I had come back after Memorial Day.

But how had it got here?

Obviously I was meant to look at it. But I didn't have a computer. The hardware remnants that Gary had left behind had been taken by the police.

Some of my friends had computers, but I couldn't ring them up and say *"Hi, I've just found a CD ROM hidden in one of my bags. I think it's been left there for me to look at. Can I come round and put it in your machine?"* God knows what virus I might be inflicting upon them. And God knows what was on the disk. Perhaps it was something that only I was meant to see.

The best thing would be for me to phone up Sergeant Wilkinson and hand it over to him, sight unseen.

And that was the thought that was in my head when I entered *Office Depot* the next day.

I had wanted a laptop anyway, I reasoned to myself, so it was not a waste of money. Think of what I could do on this! I could... I could... Well, I needed a new typewriter, if nothing else.

All the software Joe and Jill Cool could ever need (and loads of software they would never need) was already pre-installed on the laptop, so it was just a matter of fire it up and play.

Several programmes badgered me to register, but I ignored them.

It was 17:00 when I closed the drawer with CD ROM 27 inside.

It was 17:05 when I died.

Death takes many shapes and forms. It's not only cats that have nine lives, all of us die many times during our lifetimes. We die when a loved one dies; we die when a relationship ends; we die when we are rejected; we die at injustice. Every little death chips away at our soul, until that day when the soul itself gives up and leaves the body forever.

As I looked at the screen I felt myself die.

Not one death, but a death for every one of the thousand photographs that were on the disk.

Photographs of me.

Photographs of me having sex.

With men I did not know.

With men I had never met before in my life.

82

I won't describe the sordid detail of the photographs, I'll leave that to your imagination.

In a lot of the photographs I had my eyes shut (because obviously I had been unconscious). But the scariest part was that in some of them *I had my eyes open*. Looking carefully, I could see that my eyes were glazed – but to the casual student of pornography, it would seem like I was awake, knew what I was doing and was enjoying it.

I have spoken a lot in this book about my feelings. You know me by now so, again, detail is not required.

Suffice it to say that if depression was a hole, I was now at the earth's core.

It took me a long time to get hold of Sergeant Wilkinson the next morning. When he did eventually answer his cellphone, he sounded just slightly piqued when he heard who it was.

I explained about finding the disk and about what was on it. Should I bring it down to the police station? No, he would come round to collect it.

"I suppose," I said, "that it's the same on the other disks…?"

"What other disks?"

"The ones CSU took away. There were a few hundred of

them - " I was jolted as realisation hit me. Did they all contain pictures of me? Were they all copies of the same disk or were all the pictures different?

"They haven't reported back yet," explained Wilkinson. "I'll chase them up later. I'll be with you within the hour."

I was praying that he did not want to look at the contents of the disk on my laptop. The embarrassment would have been too great. But thankfully he made no mention of it.

"You all right?" Wilkinson took the disk from me. "You look pale."

"So would you be if you'd seen such pictures of yourself. But you're a man, you'd probably be proud of it."

"Sorry?"

I sighed. "No, I'm sorry. That was unfair. The thing is, I knew things were going on, I should have stopped them sooner."

His hand touched my shoulder. "And how would you have done that? This supports your contention that you were being drugged. When the results come back, we'll know what he used."

"But we can't turn back the clock, can we? What do you think he's done with these photos?"

"Carly, its best not to think about it. Maybe he's done nothing. I'll pass this to CSU for forensic examination, and we might have to get Vice involved."

"Will they want to interview me?"

"Possibly. We'll see."

"I could be out there on the internet."

"It's possible, of course. But these sort of people usually keep to themselves, either individually or in their little groups."

"Well this was certainly a group!" There was no mirth in my humour.

"Of course. Sorry." Now it was him who seemed slightly embarrassed. Strange for a man who had seen me completely naked and probed in the doctor's surgery. "I'll get back to you," he said.

I saw him out. On the landing, he stopped and took a step back towards me. He kept his voice low. "Whatever we find on these disks, whatever we find in your body, what's done is done. We know he's left the country. He's not stupid, these people never are. He won't come back. He knows we'll have him if he tries to re-enter the country."

"Can't he be extradited or something?"

He pursed his lips, thinking carefully before replying. "For what?" He tapped his pocket. "Taking pictures of his wife? Who, as you say, seems wide awake and willing? Drugging his wife? Just because there are drugs in his wife's system is not proof that he administered them. Building a case against him will be a long and painstaking process."

That really was not what I wanted to hear.

"But," he smiled comfortingly, "the process has begun. He's no longer a physical threat to you. Try to move on."

"Pick up sticks," I said.

"What?"

"Pick up the sticks of my life, sort them out, discard those I don't want, cherish those I do. And move on."

"Nice one."

"That," I said, "is easier for me to say than do."

83

It was Sergeant Wilkinson's next phone call that made me seek psychiatric help.

It was three days after he had collected the disk from me. My cellphone rang while I was on the landline to Selma at MAC to confirm that I would be returning the following Monday. After hasty goodbyes, I answered it.

"Carly, it's Roger Wilkinson."

"Hi, Roger."

"Carly, I've had the forensic report about the disks."

"Great. What did they say?"

There was a pause before he said, "Carly, they were all blank."

"What?"

"Every one of them. They had never been used."

"Well, thank God you've got the one I gave you."

Another pause. I knew what was coming, and in the name of God I didn't believe it. "Carly…"

"What?"

"That was blank as well."

84

My freefall into hell was now non-stop.

I didn't know what to do. I phoned my friends, hoping they would listen and not shut me out. They were incredulous, disbelieving – but whether it was me or the police they disbelieved was unclear. Even Jacqui, who had been my staunchest ally, had doubt in her voice.

"What are you going to do, Carls?"

I was crying. "I don't know. The police are saying I'm lying. Where can I go? Who can I turn to?"

"But they've also said he's gone."

I sniffed. "That's true. But Jac, I'm not lying. You should have seen what I saw on that disk! I was raped, many times over, by a group of about five different men."

Jacqui said nothing.

"Jac?"

"Sorry Carls, I don't know what to say. But the drugs tests will be back in three months."

"And you just know what they're going to say, don't you!"

"Carls, you're my friend. You know I'll always be there for you. But - "

"Perhaps it's time I stopped all this?"

"Well... yes. Perhaps it's time we all moved on."

"I'll phone my Mom, she'll know what to do."

She knew what to do, all right – but it wasn't what I wanted to hear.

"The way you're carrying on, Carly, you need to be in hospital with the white coats, locked up."

"Thanks Mom."

"I could have told you he was weird when you met him."

"Oh so you *do* believe me?"

"I believe you've had a rough time, dear. Obviously my words can't get you out of it, neither can your friends. Perhaps it's time you sought professional help."

Harshly put but, as always, Mom was right. I *did* need help. If only I could talk to someone, someone who hadn't heard my story before – someone who hadn't lived it with me – and who would bring an open mind to it.

We all have needs, whether it be drink, food, sex, whatever, and at one time or another we will all pay for someone to satisfy those needs (like going to a restaurant, right? What did you think I was inferring?). My need was to be listened to. And it was time to pay someone to listen to me.

As it turned out, it was three someones. Three psychiatrists in the Murray Hill area. I chose one, and then I was referred on to another then another as my story unfolded.

I was nervous the first time, but once I got into my story the relief of having someone just listen, without any preconceived judgements or opinions, was palpable.

I didn't know why I was being 'referred up' each time, I was just told "There is someone else who would like to hear your story", and dutifully I obeyed (and dutifully I paid the increasingly horrendous bills).

The third person I saw was a very pleasant man, quite elderly, who has asked – for obvious reasons – not to be named (he was, and still is, a criminal psychologist). He read my reports and listened to my story.

He gave me his verdict on a sunny July afternoon in his cosy consulting room just off Park Avenue South. I remember it well. Thick red carpet, wooden-clad walls. Not only do I remember it well because it was a nice place, but on that beautiful summer's afternoon this lovely man said some things which gave me hope, wonderful glorious hope. Hope that I was not going mad. Hope that I could come through this. Hope that there was a future.

I hadn't been expecting it. I thought he was going to tell me I was going insane.

"It is my opinion Carly that you are not delusional. Your husband is obviously a very dangerous person – but sadly there is nothing we can do about that. For all intents and purposes he has gone. I have studied these kinds of people – oh yes, there are more of them about than you realise. You've described a form of psychopath, one who is highly intelligent, motivated purely for his own ends. What ends? They vary from person to person. From what you've told me – well obviously he is bisexual. The obsession with children's things indicates a predilection for pedophilia, either nascent or actual. Pedophiles, contrary to popular belief, are not loners. They tend to sniff out – if you'll forgive the expression – their own kind. They form cliques, 'secret societies' if you will, for their own mutual ends and gratification.

"You have done well to get rid of him. It is a proven fact that pedophiles are also murderers."

It was a buoyant Carly who walked down Park Avenue later that afternoon, a Carly who at last had someone to believe her, a Carly who had been reassured that she was not going mad, a Carly who now believed she did have a future, a Carly who was so happy that she entered Lord John's Bootery over on 3rd Avenue with just one intention: to waste an inordinate amount of money on shoes. Shoes, shoes and more shoes.

And as I was looking around at the plethora of ways to blow my money, little did I realise that I was a Carly who was very soon to fall deeper than she had ever fallen in her life.

85

Two weeks later it was August. I was feeling great, I was getting my life back together, things were good. I could now say the name Gary Goffrey without wincing or shaking or crying. My freelance work was suffering a summer drought, so I had arranged to go back to MAC as vacation cover, full time for a few weeks.

It was August 3rd before I remembered that this was the month I was due to get the drugs tests back. I knew that, somehow, the tests would be negative – just like the disks had been blank. But I didn't mind, I was over it all now. Negative or positive results, who cared? Everyone kept telling me to move on, and they were right. Gary Goffrey had gone from my life and gone from the country – the test results would not alter that, whatever way they came out.

I was a human being. I was alive. That was all that mattered. I had been to hell and back. I had experienced the pits of despair. But I, Carly, had come through it. I had even started divorce proceedings. Nothing could hurt me in such a way ever again.

Little did I know.

Ho-fucking-ho.

∞

Okay, whichever way the drugs results went, it did not matter. But I needed to know the results, if only to be proved right. It was a win-win situation for me. If the results came back positive, it was proof I was right about being drugged. If they came back negative, I would also be right because that's what I had predicted.

It was the middle of August and still I had heard nothing. I had given notice on the apartment, and Jacqui and I had decided to share together. We had signed a lease on an apartment in a block near Barbara on the Upper West Side effective from October (overlooking the park – very expensive but it was about time I used Grandma's money for something). Minetta Lane and all its memories were going to be left behind me. So I needed closure.

If the police wouldn't call me, I would call them.

Somewhere deep in my purse, squashed underneath a packet of *Marlborough* and above a crumpled *Wrigley's Gum* wrapper, was Sergeant Wilkinson's card. I smoothed it out, picked up my landline phone and dialled his number.

Immediately I got the service provider's message that the phone was switched off. There was no voicemail option.

So be it, no problem, I would try him later.

I tried him three times that day, but each time the phone was switched off.

I tried him three times every day for the next week, but each time – you've guessed it.

I thought of going down to the 6th Precinct, but I didn't want to be seen to be causing a fuss. They had said they would contact me when the results were back. Poor Sergeant Wilkinson was probably on vacation or something, maybe sunning himself somewhere warm and relaxing – and there was this mad bitch ringing him to see if her test results were back!

After five weeks, I no longer got the service provider's message when I rang Wilkinson's phone. I got nothing. The day that happened was the day I decided to phone the main 6th Precinct number, not the Sergeant's cellphone. Maybe he had moved or, more mundanely, got a new phone. I could be forever phoning a now non-existent number.

An echoey Directory Assistance gave me the number.

741-4811.

A female voice answered after three rings. "6th Precinct."

"Ah, hello. I've been trying to contact Sergeant Wilkinson, I wonder if he's about?"

"Your name please ma'm?"

"Carly Goffrey."

"Your address?"

"162 Minetta Lane, apartment 3."

"And what is it in connection with?"

"You might have heard of my case. I was having problems with my husband drugging me. Gary Goffrey? My drugs tests were due back in August. Sergeant Roger Wilkinson said he would phone me, but he hasn't. Maybe he's been away or something?"

"Please hold the line ma'm?"

"Sure - " Already I was listening to nothing.

I was hanging on for ages. Perhaps I had been cut off and the police were trying to ring me back while I was sitting here like an idiot listening to an empty, echoey line.

After five minutes, I was about to put the phone down when a male voice said, "Hello, ma'm?"

"Hello?" That didn't sound like him. "Is, er, is that Sergeant Wilkinson?"

"No ma'm, this is Captain of Detectives Hood. How may I help you?"

Christ, bureaucracy, even in the police.

With a patience I did not feel, I went through my story again. Captain Hood was quiet at the end of it. I expected him to put me on hold and go check to see if the results were back. Instead he said something unexpected. "Are you at home, ma'm?"

"Yes."

"And will you be there all evening?"

"I can be."

"We would like to send one of our officers around to talk to you, would that be all right?"

Wow, what had the results shown?

"Yes, yes that would be fine. When?"

"Probably within the next two hours."

"Okay, fine."

86

I didn't know whether to be worried, pleased, elated or what. The police were coming round to see me! To interview me, I guess. So the drugs tests must have been positive after all. And perhaps at last the police would tell me what it was they knew that I didn't. What they had kept from me.

I was nervous but excited, and I had two major visits to the john in the hour it took the police to get to me.

I was busy tidying up things that didn't need to be tidied up, when the doorbell rang.

Dashing over, I snatched up the entry phone. "Hi, come on up, first floor."

"I know where it is, Carls," said a familiar voice.

"Jac?"

"I thought I'd come to see if you were all right. You haven't phoned the shop for a few days."

"Yes. Yes, I'm fine. Come on up."

Actually this could be quite good. Jac could corroborate a lot of my story. In case the police needed a witness, that sort of thing.

I explained about the police's imminent arrival as I put fresh coffee into the machine.

"So there must be something in the drugs tests," I finished.

"Seems like it."

"The good thing is, with you being here you can corroborate a lot of my story."

Jacqui picked up a cookie as the coffee began to drip through. "Sure. Sure I can." Was there a reticence in her voice? She looked up at me. "I can corroborate what you told me."

"Is there a problem?"

"No. But it's *what you told me*. Sure, I can tell them that Gary was a bit of a weirdo, but I was never a witness to any of the... stuff."

"No, that's fine. Just tell them what you know."

The doorbell rang again. This time it was the police. I buzzed them up and stood in my doorway watching as two women, just a little older than me, came up the stairs. They showed me their badges and identified themselves as Sergeant Rosemary Marinelli and Detective Collette Sanders. They had 'nice' written all over them.

They accepted my offer of coffee and sat down on the couch.

"This is my friend Jacqui," I explained as I went into the kitchen.

"That's good," said Marinelli. To Jac she said, "Have you known Mrs Goffrey long?"

"Carly, please." I called in. "Call me Carly."

"Yes, I've known her for a few years," answered Jac. "We started working in MAC together at almost the same time. MAC – the make-up company?"

The policewomen nodded.

I came in with cups, milk and sugar on a tray and a plate of Oreos. "I don't know how you take it, so you can put it in yourself."

"Thank you." Sanders leant forward and began to pour. She didn't have to ask how her boss took it.

I sat on the floor in front of them. "So, have you got the test results back? Do you want to interview me?"

Marinelli sat forward. "I know this is probably tedious, but do you mind giving us a brief outline of your story again?" Sanders had finished pouring and was pulling a notepad and pencil from her bag.

"It should all be on my file," I reasoned.

"Yes, but it's always good to hear it with the personal slant. Do you mind? Just briefly, no great detail."

So I told them the story. Was I ever tired of telling it? Not if it meant people would listen. Not if it meant people would believe me.

I left out most detail, but it still took me over an hour, two cups of coffee for all, a cigarette each for me and Jac, and nearly a whole packet of Oreos.

As I mentioned the medical and drugs tests, I asked "Is it usual for Sergeants to be there when these tests are being done?"

"Depends," said Marinelli. "Possibly, if you were a suspect."

"So I'd be naked in front of him? Sergeant Wilkinson?"

"Only in extreme circumstances if it was thought you would dispose of something before any female officer could be present. And certainly not in this case as you were the complainant not the suspect."

"So there'll be the doctor and a female officer present only?"

"Yes."

"Well, Sergeant Wilkinson stayed all the way through my examination."

"With no female officer present?"

"Only the doctor's nurse."

"I see."

"Not usual then?"

"Not usual, no."

There was a quietness in the room. Sanders finished writing on her pad and closed it up. Marinelli said, "Mrs Goffrey – Carly. We would like to interview you more formally. Would you mind? Down at the station. On record."

"On record? Isn't that just for criminals?"

"No, not at all. Yours is a most unusual story. It's so that we have a full record of it – and you will have one too, we'll give you a copy. Bring Ms Deegan with you, if you like."

"What, you want me to come now?"

"If it's convenient. It seems like the perfect time."

"At last," I muttered. I said, "Sure I'll come. You haven't told me the results of the drugs tests."

"Let's get the full story on record first."

87

Jacqui and I sat in the back of the silver Ford Taurus (did the police have a job lot of them?), Detective Sanders drove with Sergeant Marinelli next to her. I was elated. At last, after all this time, somebody was going to take down my story. In fact I was to have a copy of it on tape, which might come in useful in the future.

"I have been waiting ages for this," I said chattily. "For someone to take a statement from me."

"We'll sort it all out," reassured Marinelli.

I noticed we were heading eastwards along Bleecker Street, not west then north for the 6th Precinct. When the U-turn I expected did not occur by the next traffic lights, I asked "Aren't we going to the police station?"

"Yes, we are," explained Marinelli. "But not the 6th. We're from the 9th. Avenue C. That's where we're going."

"But the 6th is our precinct," said Jacqui. "Close to our work."

"I know," Marinelli nodded. "That's why we're not going there. If only you'd come to us straight away."

"I didn't know I could pick and chose which police I used," I said. "I thought you had to go to your local cops, like a catchment area or something."

Marinelli didn't respond.

I thought I would try again on the testing. "Can't you give me a clue as to what the drugs tests found? Must be something major, hmm?"

"We'll get to that later. First we want your story. Every single detail." Marinelli looked from one to the other of us. "You'd best be prepared. This could well be a long night."

Marinelli was not wrong.

We arrived at 130 Avenue C at 19:00. There was the usual hustle and bustle of any inner city police station, but we were buzzed through into the relative peace and quiet of the interview rooms, well away from the front desk area.

It was exactly like you see on TV. Marinelli and Sanders sat on one side of a small wooden table, Jac and I sat the other. There was a huge mirror on the wall, behind which sat who knew who. In the corner up above, the Cyclops eye of a camera stared down onto the room.

Marinelli offered, and we accepted, refreshments, and Sanders went out. Marinelli asked us not to talk about my story until the recording equipment was switched on, so we spoke about – what else? – make-up. I had just promised the Sergeant some free samples if she would care to pop into the shop sometime, when Sanders came back in carrying a tray with four brews of indeterminate warm brown liquid, two packets of eat-by-that-date sandwiches and some shortbread cookies.

Marinelli waited through the rustling of cellophane and the first tentative slurps of the liquid (no, sorry, I could not tell you what it was), and then she said "Right. Ready?"

"As I'll ever be."

"Now, we want you to tell us everything. A bit of background from your childhood and then from the time you first met him until this very moment. Tell us things just as they happened, don't embellish but leave nothing out, no matter how trivial it may seem. We want it all recorded. Can you do that?"

"Yes," I nodded. This was what I had wanted for a long time, and yet suddenly I was afraid of my memories, afraid of the long-buried demons that might resurface. "Yes, I can."

"Okay then." Marinelli nodded towards the mirror.

I took a deep breath.

It took me four hours. *Four hours.* Including one pee and two cigarette breaks.

Other than the occasional verification and prompting by Jacqui, it was a monologue. A soliloquy. A valediction to my life with Gary Goffrey. The policewomen did not question or interrupt.

At the end the four of us just sat there. After a while Marinelli nodded towards the mirror.

My palms were sweaty, even shaking a little. I was experiencing a pernicious dichotomy. On the one hand, I was shocked at the extent, the quantity and the detail of my recollections. In four hours I had relived and re-experienced almost four years with Gary Goffrey. On the other hand, hearing it now set out all at once and in gory detail, I could well understand how some people thought I might be making it up or embellishing and twisting and exaggerating incidents. Believe me, I wasn't. But what would a Devil's Advocate see? Quite simply, a woman who had married in haste, had discovered she disliked her husband and his Little Ways, had finally driven him away – and now had the rest of her life to repent at leisure.

I raised my head and looked over at the two policewomen. I wanted to say "What do you think?", but I didn't. Instead, I sighed and said "Can you tell me my results now?"

88

It was a moment or two before Marinelli answered. She looked at Sanders, who nodded, and then she looked over to me. "We need to have a chat with someone. Shouldn't take us long. You ladies stretch your legs or something." With that the two policewomen stood up and left the room.

I took the advice and stood up and stretched. "Christ, I could do with a cigarette."

My saviour as ever, Jacqui produced her *Benson & Hedges*. We lit up.

"How do you think it went?" I asked.

She shrugged. "You held nothing back, just like they wanted. Some of that even I did not know."

"But did it sound stupid, like I was making it up? Or was it believable?"

Jacqui took a long drag. "It sounded… weird. Which is exactly what your relationship was, wasn't it?"

My turn to drag. "And then some. I wish they'd give me my damn test results, though."

The door opened and Sanders came back in. "She won't be long," she nodded back at the door. "Just making a phone call." She shook her head at Jacqui's offer of a cigarette.

Two minutes later, Marinelli was back. I had hoped she

would be carrying a clipboard or a file or something with my results in, but she brought nothing with her. "Someone wants to talk to you," she said. "If you wouldn't mind waiting, he's driving over."

"Driving over?"

"From Federal Plaza."

I looked at my watch. It was midnight. I know one always thinks of oneself as the centre of the world, but what was so important that someone from Federal Plaza – the FBI – wanted to see me at this hour? What couldn't wait until the next morning? What did they know?

"Yes, we'll wait," I said.

89

Marinelli must have received a cue from somewhere, perhaps a beep or vibration from her pocket, because forty minutes later she announced "He's here," and she stood up and left the room. It was another twenty minutes before she came back. She was accompanied by a big, stout man, slightly ruddy cheeks, black hair greying at the temples.

Despite the hour and his hasty appearance, he was wearing a shirt and tie, grey suit trousers but no jacket. He introduced himself as Special Agent Patrick. I presumed that was his surname.

His smile was friendly, but with that hint of suspicion that law enforcement officers just cannot shake off, be they young, old, serving or retired, police, FBI, you name it.

He sat down in Marinelli's chair. "I want to thank you ladies for coming here tonight. Rosemary has given me an outline of your story, but I will need to hear it for myself. I'll watch the video over the next few hours. But that's no reason to detain you."

"What about my test results?" I asked.

He seemed not to hear me. "It's obvious the story has already unravelled itself. We would like to investigate this as much as we can, but I have two problems. Your husband has left the country. It's a pity but it's a fact. So what would be the point of investigating something when there would be no end result? The most we could hope for would be to have him detained if he ever tries to set foot on US soil again - and he's already on the list. Your testimony will be a great help." His avuncular smile seemed to indicate that that was that.

"And what's the other one?" I asked. "You said you had two problems."

Patrick sighed and looked up at Marinelli. She gave a shrug. Patrick looked back at me and was quiet for a few moments, as if making up his mind. He breathed out slowly, his cheeks puffing.

"You have asked about your test results."

"Yes, I was told it would be four months. They were due back in August."

Another pause, then he said "There are none."

"Oh, they were negative?"

"No, there are none. There are no results."

I was aware that Marinelli had stepped closer to me.

"I'm sorry," I said. "I don't understand."

"There are no results because there was never a test."

My guts clenched. "What the hell are you talking about?" My voice was raised. "I had a test." I turned sharply. "Jac, you were there, you were with me."

My friend was frowning. "No, that wasn't me, that was Jenny. But she said she didn't actually go in with you. You went in on your own."

I turned back. "This is fucking ridiculous, what do you mean there was never a test?" Now I was shouting.

Marinelli put her hand on my shoulder as Patrick raised his hands to quieten me down. Tears began to fall down my cheeks.

"How did you first contact Sergeant Wilkinson?"

"He..." I thought back. "He telephoned me."

"So he first contacted you?"

"Yes, but I was about to go to the police anyway."

"But you never did."

"Never did what?"

"Go to the police."

"Well, I didn't have to, did I? They contacted me."

"And he showed you identification?"

"Of... course."

"And so did the other police officers? The CSU people?"

"Yes – well, I think they did..."

"And when you rang Sergeant Wilkinson?"

"It was the number on his card. His cellphone."

"So you never actually phoned the 6th Precinct?"

Oh no.

"And you never went to the station house?"

Oh no, oh no, oh no.

I swallowed hard. "What... what are you telling me?"

He took a deep breath before saying, "Carly, I'm sorry to have to tell you this. But there is no Sergeant Wilkinson at the 6th Precinct. Or anywhere else. And there is no CSU team at West 10th Street, they don't have them at local level. There is no Doctor Wang who works for the police. We will go round to the address you gave us, but it's more than likely we'll find empty premises. The first time the police had any involvement in your story is when you phoned them asking for Sergeant Roger Wilkinson. That name is on a national wanted list. They contacted us.

"You have been conned, Mrs Goffrey. And it sounds like you have been used as well."

I was suddenly aware of the table coming up towards my head. I can just remember the scrape of the edge against my hairline, which cut me and gave me a scar which I still carry to this day. I was not aware of the thump as my head bounced, and I was unconscious by the time my body had crumpled to the floor.

90

They wanted to keep me in hospital overnight, but I wasn't having any of it. If I stayed there, who knows what would happen? I might be sectioned as a mad woman. The woman who made up stories about her husband, who accused him of taking pictures of her, who made up a whole police investigation which never happened. Even her own mother had told her she needed help.

I allowed them to stitch me (shaving a couple of inches off my hairline in the process) and then I insisted I left. I signed whatever forms they put in front of me and, linking arms with Jacqui and on slightly wobbly feet, I left at 05:30.

A cab took us back to Minetta Lane, and I stood in the front staring up at the place. The place where I had been used. The place where I had been abused. The place where I had been gang raped, sodomised and degraded – without my knowledge.

The place where I had been betrayed.

"Are you sure you want to go in?" asked Jacqui.

I looked up at the windows of my apartment. I fully expected to see him standing there with that inane little boy grin, waving. But the windows just stared back at me, as empty as my life felt right now.

"Yes," I said. "I must."

Inside, the apartment was the same as it had been since he left. No feeling of a malign presence, nothing. But it seemed like I had been away ages, not just a few hours. It was the feeling you get when you come back from a long trip, the feeling that the place is yours but it isn't, that you have to get to know it all over again.

"Coffee?" Jacqui went into the kitchen, leaving a dazed Carly standing in the living room.

"Yeh. Thanks."

I must have time-jumped because she was back instantly, two mugs in her hands. "Here. Sit down," she said gently.

I did as I was told. I looked at my dear, dear friend. "Jac, I just can't believe it. Are they saying I made everything up?" I took a cigarette from her packet.

"They're not saying that, Carls."

"But I bet they're thinking it." I touched my stitches with my hand and immediately regretted it. The tablets they had given me at the hospital had stopped the headache, but the pain from the tear was raw.

"They're saying that last night was the first time the police have been involved," said Jacqui. "That Wilkinson and the rest of them weren't real. It was an elaborate game, a con."

"Which I could have made up. They'll be doing me for wasting police time."

"No they won't. I am a witness, remember? I saw Wilkinson. Jenny and Helena saw the policemen too. Jenny went with you to Doctor Wang's."

That brightened me up. "You did, didn't you? And so did they. Thank God for you, thank God for my friends." The coffee was strong and black, and as Jacqui liked to say "The opposite of the men you date!"

I dragged a full half inch off my cigarette. "So what happens now, do you think?"

"They said they would be in contact again."

"Four months like last time? But that wasn't them, was it?"

Jacqui just shook her head. "It's hard to get your head round. Even I can't believe it. Really it's now just a matter of moving forward. Of - " She made quotation marks with her fingers. "'Getting on with your life'."

"I feel utterly… zero. At rock bottom. Deflated."

"I know you must."

"Will you stay? I don't think I can be on my own at the moment."

"Of course I will. But why don't you come and stay with me?"

I looked at her.

"Leave here," she continued. "Forever. Make the new start, don't wait until October. A new life as from now. Put all this behind you."

"I… I… That sounds good. But I can't think straight at the moment."

"You should rest."

"Yes, I should." I drained my coffee and stubbed the butt in the ashtray.

At the bedroom door, I stopped. "But not here." I turned back. "I can't stay here. Thank you, Jac. Yes, I'll come with you."

My friend picked up her cellphone and dialled a cab.

Twenty minutes later we left.

And I never, ever went back to 162 Minetta Lane.

91

Jac and some other friends moved my stuff for me, bit by bit over the coming weeks. I was now at the lowest point of my life, the nadir of my existence.

They let me have my time, they let me have my space. They did all they could for me. The direction I now travelled was up to me. I contemplated suicide, but that would have meant Gary Goffrey and his cohorts had won.

The only advantage of being at a nadir is that there is only one way to go: up. I was at the bottom of a deep pit. There was no instant ladder to get me out of it, save for the one that I could make for myself.

Slowly, slowly, rung by rung, I made that ladder.

I chose life.

Two weeks on. I hadn't returned to work. MAC were being very good, they said I could come back when I felt up to it. I had told my agency to put my freelance work on hold.

I was well ensconced with Jacqui in her apartment. We had done some washing the previous night, and before she had gone out to work that morning Jac had sorted the stuff into her pile and my pile.

I found a black top and bra which were not mine, they looked like they should be part of Jac's MAC uniform. I placed them on her pile.

I thought nothing more of it until I went into my bedroom that evening and found them back on my bed.

Jac was watching TV and eating a plate of spag bol.

"Jac, you've left that top and bra on my bed." I carried the items into the living room.

"They're yours, not mine."

"No, they're not mine…"

Jac stopped eating and turned towards me. I was holding out the top. "Not mine," she confirmed.

"We should be able to tell from the size - " I gave a small gasp.

"Carls, what is it?"

"There… there's no label."

"What about the bra?"

I threw the top onto the couch next to Jac and stretched out the bra. "My God, look at the size of it! We could both get our tits in that and still have room for a family of immigrants."

"No label?"

"No label."

"These were with your clothes I brought from the apartment."

"Clothes with no label," I spoke softly. "He used to do that. Cut labels out of clothes."

Jac said nothing.

Time was, I would have gone hysterical. But this was the new, practical Carly.

"I think," I said, "I'll phone the police."

I spoke to Rosemary Marinelli and told her what we had found.

"Have you let anyone know where you are living?" she asked.

"My friends, my family, obviously. And you. But none of his friends. I've had no contact with them."

"Keep it that way. You're sure these things were brought from your apartment?"

"Sure, but not positive."

"Chances are they're just remnants from the past which were in a drawer and forgotten. If he had tried to come back into the country, we would have been notified, but I'll check just in case."

She was back on the phone within the hour. "No, he's not here. He's still in Australia as far as we can tell. The clothes are probably just a throwback, like we said."

"Thank God for that."

"Carly, while I've got you, we need to have another talk. Can we meet?"

"You can come round if you like."

"Tomorrow morning? Will you be on your own?"

"Yes, Jacqui will be at work."

"Fine. Around eleven?"

"Eleven tomorrow, okay."

That would give me time to do something I had been meaning to do for a while.

92

There is a fifteen to seventeen hour time difference between the US and Australia. Therefore if you want to phone that country, and vice versa, you have to phone in the middle of the night to catch them in the middle of their day.

It was midnight when I picked up the phone. Jac was fast asleep and snoring in her room (go girl, chop down those trees).

It took a few seconds to connect, but then the line started ringing. It rang and rang. Maybe I had the wrong number.

Then an old lady answered. The connection was good and it sounded like she was with me in the room, not twelve thousand miles away.

"Oh hello," I put on my bright and breezy voice, Ms Efficiency. "Can I speak to Gary please?"

"Who is it?" asked the kindly voice.

"Just a friend."

"I'm not too sure if he's here at the moment."

"Why don't you go and have a little look around and see if you can see him?"

"Oh yes, okay."

There was a clunk as she put the phoned down. I could hear distant movement as I waited. It was two minutes before she came back.

"Hello?"

"Hello."

"I've had a little look around everywhere, and you know what?"

"What?"

"I couldn't see him anywhere. He could be out with his new lady friend."

"Is that Mrs Goffrey?"

"Yes, it is."

"We've never met. This is his wife in New York."

There was silence. Then: "His wife?"

"His wife of four years. Another Mrs Goffrey. Perhaps you could tell your precious Angel Baby when he comes back that the FBI are after him? And if ever I see him again, it won't be the FBI he will have to worry about - one of us won't leave alive. Thanks very much. Goodbye."

93

Jacqui went off to work as normal the next morning. I had debated whether to tell my friend that the police were coming round, but Marinelli had indicated that she wanted me to be on my own, and I knew Jac would only insist on staying if I told her.

On the dot of 11:00, the doorbell rang. I picked up some mail that was on the doormat and then looked through the peephole. Marinelli.

"Hi."

"Hi Carly." She came in and I held the door open for a moment in case there was anyone else with her.

"You on your own?" I asked.

"Yes. This is… sort of unofficial."

"Well go through and sit down. Coffee?"

"Thank you, no."

She went into the living room and sat down on the couch. I sat on a single armchair.

"How are you? How's your head?" she asked.

"I'm not bad. The head's okay. Worst part was when I had the stitches out."

"The hair's growing back already."

"Thank God. I didn't want that reminder there the rest of my life. Soon the scar will be covered over. But *I'll* know it's there and I'll know how I got it. The lasting legacy of a marriage gone bad."

"Don't be hard on yourself."

"Why not? I was the one who was a fool. A complete fool."

She shook her head. "You were not. It could have happened to anybody. You just happened to be the one they picked."

I paused. *"They?"*

"There are some things I must tell you. Agent Patrick doesn't know I'm here. He wanted to leave things as they were. Thought you'd get over it. Which you will, but it would be unfair for you not to know everything."

I felt a small trembling in my guts. What did she have to tell me? And did I want to hear it?

"Sure you won't have a coffee?" I asked. "I think I need one."

She smiled. "Okay then. Why not?" She got up and followed me into the kitchen. "We told you that the first time we heard your story was when you contacted us asking for this Sergeant Wilkinson."

I filled the coffee machine. "Yep."

"Well that was true. Agent Patrick mentioned about Wilkinson being on the national wanted list. What we didn't tell you was that your husband and all his other friends were already on the FBI files and were under investigation too."

I didn't turn around as the *Costa Rica El Portillo* started to drip through. "For what?" I opened the wall cupboard door to put the coffee tin away.

"Child pornography."

There was a loud bang as I dropped the tin onto the work surface. Thankfully it didn't break, and I put the lid back on quickly. "You… you mean pedophiles?"

"Yes."

I stared at the coffee machine. After a while, I said "Go on."

"The thing about pedophile rings is that they are very clever. They operate under cover of normality. Often they are, or they pretend to be, happily married men. And sometimes women as well."

"*Women?*"

"Believe it. And they rarely get caught. Don't believe all this hype about the people who are found out downloading internet porn, they are just schmucks. Real pedophiles don't confine themselves to looking at a screen…"

Her words hung in the air as I took the jug from the machine and poured. "Milk?"

"Just as it comes, thanks."

"Let's go back inside." A packet of chocolate chip cookies had somehow appeared in my hand, so I put them on the coffee table, grabbing three for myself.

"They cover their tracks," continued Marinelli. "They operate in groups. Membership of the groups is strictly limited to their own kind, and every one is heavily vetted. Like the masons or the local lodge, only much more harder to get into. That's why we can rarely infiltrate them. And that's why most child disappearances go unsolved. If a child's body turns up, then we have some evidence, forensics and all that. But often the children go missing, never to be seen again."

I crammed two cookies into my mouth to try to stop the nausea that was rising. "And Gary?"

"George Goffrey was in the thick of it. He was a core member of a group set up over ten years ago, when he was first in the country. Things got hot for him then, and he went home to Australia. Then after many years, he misbehaved there, he thought the net was closing and he got out again and came back. It didn't take him long to revive the old group. They thought they were untouchable. They got away with their perversions all those years ago and they thought they could get away with them again."

"And did they? Get away with them again?"

"You don't want to know." She saw my look of anguish. "Yes, they did."

I leant forward, my head in my hands. "And what about me? How do I fit into all this?"

"You were his cover. His wife. True love. How could a man just married, bowled over by love, his *coup de foudre*, possibly be a pedophile?"

"But the things that happened to me...?"

She thought before she continued. "Pedophilia is a sexual perversion. But it's the *sexual* that is the imperative. Children are not their exclusive prey. Sexual deviation and satisfaction is. If you don't mind me saying so, have you considered yourself? What you look like?"

My hands were clammy, my arms were pale. I felt as if all the blood had drained out of my body. Standing up, I went over to the mirror on the wall.

And there I was, staring back at myself.

Why hadn't I seen it before?

My hair was longer now, but I often wore it short. It was very short when he met me, I remember noticing that his hair was longer than mine. My breasts had always been small, almost non-existent. Vanity made me buy bras, not necessity. I was slim, often skinny – especially after I had had one of my many bouts of illness.

I could be mistaken for a boy, especially in somebody's fantasies.

94

I felt my knees begin to buckle. No, no, no, I wouldn't do this. I was *not* going to collapse again.

I said, "I always used to get ill when I put on weight. It was him, wasn't it? Keeping me skinny."

Marinelli shrugged. "They used you. They conned you. They drugged you. They took pictures of you, for their own pleasure and probably for sale as well. I wouldn't look on the internet if I was you."

"I wouldn't know *where* to look. Normal people don't." I sat back down again and took another couple of cookies. "But what about all the drug testing stuff?"

"Just a continuation. There's a great demand for pictures of gynaecological examinations."

"You mean I was being photographed?"

"They probably had a small camera set up somewhere. Maybe more than one."

I thought back to the unusual position I had had to adopt during the examination: on my knees instead of on my back. For obvious reasons, but also perhaps had I been on my back I would have spotted their camera. "And the pretending to be police?"

"You threatened to go to the police. They couldn't have that, they could not draw attention to themselves. How better to stop you than to make you believe you *had* contacted us?"

"Christ."

"But you remained a threat. They couldn't dispose of *you*, the wife of one of them. Again that would bring the police down on them. So they decided to go underground again. George Goffrey left the country, and his friends came in to tidy up after him."

"Then the disks they took away...?"

"Were no doubt full of pictures, of you and maybe of others."

"And they then said I would have to wait four months for the drugs tests to come back - "

"Four months for them to wrap up their current operations and get away, go underground, go to hell, wherever these perverts live."

"And you haven't got any of them?"

"We know names. Two of them lived downstairs in Minetta Lane."

I thought of Carlos and Michael, the two gays who had moved out just before Gary had gone. And of the keys found in their apartment.

"As I said, we have no proof of anything," continued Marinelli. "Even your testimony is your word against theirs. We don't have one computer disk with any pictures on."

"Clever."

"We like to think of it more as evil."

"And they've all gotten away."

"Bar one."

"Oh?"

"Do you know a photographer called Clive Collins?"

"Clive! Of course I do. I've worked with him on a few things. He was the one who introduced..." No, not Clive.

"He hanged himself two days ago. After the FBI had been round to interview him. They had nothing on him, even after the interview. But he took the devil's solution anyway."

I said nothing. What else was there to say? Staring at the carpet, I heard a voice, which could have been mine, say "Three and a half years…"

Marinelli finished her coffee and put her mug on the table.

"I want to thank you."

I looked up. "Thank *me*?"

"Yes. We could do nothing about them, but you scared them off. Once you threatened to go to the police because of your husband's weird behaviour."

"And I didn't even know. I thought he was just a psychopath."

"Oh, he is. All pedophiles are."

"And he won't come back?"

"Not to you. You're safe. You can get on with your life. They checked him out in Australia, and they're keeping an eye on him. But again, they have no evidence. There are so many of these clever bastards around. You wait, he'll lay low now for a few years. When he realises no one is after him, he'll resurface. Here, there, somewhere in the world. The group will reconvene, *sans* Clive Collins, or he might start a new one. And it will start all over again."

95

Did you expect me to go into a state of catatonia? Or to plunge into yet another deep depression? To go knocking on the gates of hell? To shut myself away for weeks, months, years and become the timid, used and abused little girl too shy to face the world?

Been there, done that.

This time the revelations were a relief. I had known I had not been imagining things, I had known something was wrong – I just didn't know how wrong. To have my worst fears – and literally my worst nightmares – confirmed, was like having a ten ton weight lifted from my shoulders.

Did you ever practise levitation at school? I'm sure you must have. You know, when four or five of you press down hard on somebody's shoulders and head for fifteen seconds, then suddenly take the pressure away to make the counteracting body force the pressure back outwards and you can lift the subject off the chair just by putting your index fingers under their legs and arms? That's what it felt like. I felt liberated. Justified.

Marinelli left, with promises that she would keep in touch to see how I was getting along (to see if I could progress their case further, more likely), and I went back into the living room.

Something was different in the room, in Jac's apartment. To confirm my feelings, I went and looked out of the window. Over the rooftops, I could see Brooklyn Bridge beyond.

I could see color. After years of living in a grey, sombre world, I could see color again.

I was elated. Elated enough to finish the packet of chocolate chip cookies, have two cigarettes back to back, and down another two strong cups of *El Portillo*. I didn't feel bad – I'd had a three and a half year guilt trip. From now on, my life was for me. I would live how I wanted to, do what I wanted to do. Indulge in whatever I wanted to indulge in.

Tonight I would have the biggest, fattest, most stuffed item Joe's Pizza could offer. I might even have two. It was about time I put on some weight. I'll show them who looked like a boy!

Perhaps I should have a breast enhancement?

On the table were the letters I had picked up from the front door mat earlier. One circular, one brown envelope addressed to Jac – and a white envelope for me. It had been addressed to 162 Minetta Lane and had been redirected by the mail redirection service.

The postmark was Essex County, Massachusetts, and I recognised the writing. It was from my Mom. Strange, why should she been writing to me? We had sort of fallen out after she had said the men in the white coats would be coming for me (well, you would, wouldn't you?), so a communication from her was the last thing I expected.

I settled down, cigarette in hand, coffee on the table.

There were two pieces of paper inside the envelope. The top one was a letter.

Mom said that she was upset that I had not contacted her and that I had not replied to her letters (True. Sorry Mom, kids are like that, whatever age they are). She was very concerned about me and she had been to see a psychic whom she had met through her sister. The psychic's name was Myra ("A lovely lady, you will like her"), and Mom said Myra wanted to speak to me urgently, because she could help me.

To convince me that she was genuine, Myra had given Mom a little note to give to me, as enclosed. It read:

Had your daughter not left the night that she did, she would have been murdered by her husband. A child's orange coat was found in the apartment.

96

Myra's lived in Salem, in a small house out near Lynch Park. I expected some sort of witch's cottage, with black cats roaming everywhere, dead crows hanging up, pentangles, crystal balls, backwards-written invocations on every wall – but there was none of that. It was just a small, old colonial-style house, well tended front garden, windows maybe in need of a lick of paint – in fact, it had 'normal' written all over it. She even had a satellite TV dish!

And Myra was normal too. I expected some wide-eyed, Cassandra-type woman, dressed in black, who spoke permanently in whining riddles, but she was like everyone's favourite sister or favourite aunt, depending how old you are.

We shook hands, and I felt an energy pass between us. She greeted my Mom and me and encouraged us inside. The internal decoration and furniture were in keeping with the place: simple colonial, no horned devils on the walls or snakes sliding around our feet. Not even a black cat!

"I'm so, so pleased to meet you, Carly. Thank you for coming." Myra led us through into the kitchen, which looked out over a long garden at the back.

"It's my, er…" I hesitated on the word 'pleasure'.

"Tea? It's in the pot."

"Yes. Thank you."

At her bidding we sat down at a large pine dining table. A plate of Digestive cookies was already there, and Myra brought over china cups and saucers, and then a tea pot with a knitted cosy covering it. Milk was in a separate china jug.

She sat down between me and Mom.

"I love your garden," I said, a tad nervously. I nodded out the kitchen window.

"Yes, it's lovely at this time of year," Myra sipped her tea. "What are your favourite flowers, Carly?"

I bit into a Digestive (it all helps with the weight-gain programme). "Hmm. Something I've never really thought about. I like roses, I suppose."

"Perennials. And roses are one of the oldest flowers. They can be strong, resistant to attack, resilient. Cut them down, they grow again stronger. When you think they are finished, they often aren't. Like you."

Before I could say anything, she went on. "I had difficulty when your Mom first came to me. I thought the spirit world was playing tricks on me – they do, you know."

"Really?" I hope I didn't sound too cynical.

"All the time. Often they're mischief-makers, just having fun."

"Having fun?" I was dunking Digestive number two into my tea.

"The spirit world is not wreathed in darkness you know. They like to enjoy themselves as much as we do. But it felt odd as soon as your Mom came to me. I couldn't believe what I was seeing… Perversion, rape, torture. Some extremely sick things."

"That's what Carly had been implying," my Mom's voice was hoarse, like she had a dry mouth. "But I didn't listen to her." She reached out and touched my hand. "I'm so sorry, darling."

I turned to Myra before it got too mawkish. "What happens now? Do you, er…" I waved my hand. How could I say do you go into a trance? Do you throw your head back and speak in an alien voice? Does ectoplasm rise from your mouth and fill the room? It wouldn't be polite.

"They're with me already. My friends from the other side," she spoke softly, kindly. "They just need us to be quiet for a moment. Take my hand."

Mom reached out, but she was ignored. Myra cupped my right hand between both of hers. Her hands were warm but dry. It felt comforting. She spoke normally. "This group of men are evil – but they have left you now. They have dispersed. I see... Is it the letter E?... No, no, it's a G. The letter G. He is the worst. He has been evil for so, so long. I see children – a child. Death. An unwilling death. A murder. I am moving, shaking. Where... Where am I? What are you telling me...? A train! I am on a train. It is a long time ago. Years... Ten years... They are taking me. Where's my Mommy...? Please, no. Don't break the horsey... I'll be good. I'll be quiet."

Myra closed her eyes. Slowly a tear rolled down her left cheek. She maintained the hold on my hand. It had tightened as she was speaking but now it relaxed again.

She spoke again. "Already he has been on the move, but far, far away. But he won't ever harm you, you'll be okay. It will end, but not for a few years. But I think you will hear from the police again about him. It is not going to be nice, it will be quite sick, but then that will be the end of it. But you're going to be okay because you're going to be in a nice, steady relationship. You will find happiness, Carly. And your story will be told."

I felt her relax completely, and I realised I had had my eyes closed. I opened them as she let go of my hand. She was looking at me, her eyes holding all the kindness in the world. I felt tranquillity. She asked, "Does any of that make any sense to you?"

I left Myra and Mom talking like old friends, exchanging gossip, moaning about the price of bread. Water was on the boil for a second pot of tea.

Outside, in the front garden, the sun was shining. The warm, life-affirming rays caressed my face. I could hear the seagulls out in Beverly Harbor.

I looked at the wild poppies growing haphazardly in the borders of the garden. Amongst the roses.

The nearest rose was a deep golden colour, its perfume transcending anything that could be fabricated by humans. As I put my nose close and inhaled I noticed two small sticks on the ground, the kind a bird may have dropped on the way to building its nest.

I bent down and picked them up.

I smiled.

5 years later

It had been a long journey from Florida.

First the drive in the hire car from his home in Sweetmeadow Circle, Sarasota, to Orlando International Airport, then the *United Airlines* flight to Los Angeles, arriving with two hours to spare before the *Qantas* flight to Sydney even checked in. Enough time for him to change his appearance to match the Australian passport.

The passport said his name was Ian Ramsey. He was a man of medium height, face still boyish even though he was in his fifties, short curly hair (originally dark but now dyed blond) pushed back and now receding slightly at the temples. The story was that he had been in Los Angeles on business (something in the movie industry) and was now returning home after three weeks.

Qantas made good time but the flight still took over ten hours – alleviated to an extent by his position in Business Class.

As with any country, returning nationals are not scrutinised so carefully at Immigration, so entry was a formality. Customs actually stopped him, which was irksome, but some polite answers to peremptory questions and a cursory search of his one suitcase convinced them that he was who he said he was and no he was not smuggling drugs.

Soon he was checking into the Sydney Hilton for an overnight rest before his onward flight in the morning.

∞

That evening, Ramsey met someone by pre-arrangement in one of the hotel's bars. They greeted each other like old friends, even though they had never met before and never would again. It took three drinks and an hour and a half for them to catch up on old times, and then the old friend left.

During the meeting, two packages had been exchanged. The old friend took away with him a bulky envelope which felt as if it was full of paper. Ramsey went back up to his room with a package containing a much harder object.

The next day, the *Ansett* flight took off fifteen minutes late for its one hour flight to Canberra - but Ramsey did not mind, he was not on a schedule. This one, unusually, was personal.

Ramsey left the terminal at Canberra Airport looking like a man who knew where he was going. But as he headed for the short-term car park his eyes were scanning, evaluating, choosing.

He settled on a grey Hyundai. It had only recently been parked, he could still see the heat waves rising from the bonnet. The engine would be warmed-up and ready to go.

He took a small, hard plastic tool from his pocket. A curious little object, with the numbers zero to nine scaled on the side with three slides underneath. He moved the three small slides until they married up with the numbers 343 – the code for Hyundai. Then he simply used the tool as a key and entered the vehicle.

The same key started the engine, and within seconds he was pulling up to the exit gates. He had already purchased a maximum priced parking ticket from the 'Lost tickets' button at the machine in the airport terminal, and in a moment the gates had risen and he was en route for the short drive to Holt.

Templeton Street was typical of Australian suburbia. Detached wooden and brick houses lining a wide street, neatly manicured front lawns, cars parked outside garages.

Ramsey cruised along slowly until he found the one he wanted. There were no cars parked outside this one, so he had close access. He parked, then reached across to the passenger seat, opened the new leather briefcase and took out one of the two things inside: a pair of sunglasses.

A casual observer would then have seen a slightly chubby, blond but balding man get out of the vehicle, wearing sunglasses and dressed in fawn trousers, white short-sleeved shirt, brown tie. He carried a briefcase, but instead of carrying it by the handle he had it cradled under his left arm. He looked like some sort of salesman.

What the casual observer would not have noticed was that the engine of the car had been left running.

The front door bell ding-donged in pure, twee, suburban fashion. The ring echoed for a moment and then all was quiet. The salesman stood there patiently. He knew his client was in, a phone call just ten minutes ago had confirmed it.

He did not hear any sound from behind the door, but then he became aware of a presence as someone approached from the inside. He adjusted the briefcase under his arm and opened the catches.

The door opened slowly. The person standing there was wearing a flower-patterned pink cotton mini dress. Strong, tanned legs led down to garish red high heels. The face was far too heavily made-up, but it fitted in with the persona created by the obvious platinum blonde wig.

"Yes?" The voice was deep but not without sensuality.

Ramsey said, "Good morning, Mr Goffrey?"

The head pulled back as if he had been slapped in the face. The platinum blonde wig actually jumped a little. Ramsey just stood there smiling.

The other person frowned and something flashed in the striking green eyes. It wasn't fear. It was evil. "No, sorry, you must have the wrong address. There's no one by that name here."

Tolerantly, the salesman shook his head. "I don't think so." His hand went into the open top of his briefcase. "Your name is Gary Goffrey."

"No, my name is Carlson. Georgette Carlson." He tried to close the door but the salesman's foot was in the way.

"Whatever," nodded the salesman, "that's close enough." From the briefcase he withdrew a Heckler & Koch P7 handgun, a bulbous Israeli-made silencer on the end.

The evil eyes of Gary Goffrey only had time to register the action before three bullets blasted away his face.

Revenge is now mine

Georgie fell backwards with force, a force so great it felt like he had been ripped apart. His mouth was open and his eyes were staring in shock. He saw a bloodied blonde wig fly across the floor.

He saw the man at the door turn and walk away. Then he looked down.

Daddy was lying on the floor. He was not moving.

And Daddy no longer had a face.

What had happened? *Daddy? Daddy, don't leave me! Please, Daddy, please. I don't want to be on my own again.*

He tried to bend down to shake Daddy, but he could not. Georgie looked down. He wanted to sit in a corner and hug his knees, but he could not - his knees were not there. Neither was the rest of him. Had he become invisible? Had he *always* been invisible?

Daddy was leaving him. There was nobody else he could inhabit.

He had never felt so abandoned and so alone. Not since he had watched Mommy go into the toilet on the train and this man had come along and taken him. Taken him to his friends who had abused him and murdered him.

It was all too much for a dead four year old boy to understand. He felt confused, disorientated. Cut off.

Was the 'rushower' over yet?

Where was Mommy?

Don't break the horsey!

Hurt the bitch, Daddy.

He began to cry. He could not understand what was happening.

Somebody help me, please.

Please don't leave me, Daddy.

DAVID CULLEN

THE EYE OF MAKARIOS

IN A WORLD OF TERROR THE ONLY TRUTH IS BETRAYAL

THE EYE OF MAKARIOS

David Cullen

1974. A world in turmoil. Terrorism is rife.

In the Middle East, *El Fateh* plan their first nuclear strike. The Irshman, their hardware supplier, wants a very special item in payment.

In the Mediterranean, Cyprus is an island about to be divided. Resistance leader Grivas is dying. He wants to hit his enemy from beyond the grave.

In Israel, the security services want to finish off their enemies once and for all.

In Europe, Sally wants to find her missing lover.

In a world about to implode, they all have one common link:

THE EYE OF MAKARIOS

ISBN: 978-0-9559911-0-3

Available from *amazon, Lulu* and other online booksellers and thru all good bookshops.

DAVID CULLEN

THE MESRINE CONCLUSION

ONLY ONE MAN CAN RETRIEVE THE SECRET - IF HE CAN STAY ALIVE

THE MESRINE CONCLUSION

David Cullen

1978. Only two people still alive know the explosive dark secret of the British Royal House of Windsor.

One lies in her dotage in France, the other continues to rule the royal household in Britain as she has done for 40 years.

A robbery in Paris. The secret is stolen. It must be found at all costs. Police enquiries draw a blank. They need help. There is only one man with the skills to locate the secret – Jacques Mesrine, France's Public Enemy Number One.

But there are those that want the secret for themselves and others who will stop at nothing to ensure the secret remains hidden.

Can Mesrine find the secret before the hunters find him? Death, treachery and double-cross all lead to

THE MESRINE CONCLUSION

ISBN: 978-0-9559911-1-0

Available from *amazon, Lulu* and other online booksellers and thru all good bookshops.

DAVID CULLEN

THE WINDSOR SECRET

ANYONE WHO KNOWS THE SECRET, DIES - ANYONE

THE WINDSOR SECRET

David Cullen

1997. Three women are out for revenge.

In Greece, a lover discovers that justice has not been done.
In England, a princess seeks to humiliate her ex-husband.
In France, a daughter vows retribution after eighteen years.

A secret which they thought was buried forever comes back to haunt the British Royal House of Windsor. And the deaths must start again.

And this time to preserve the secret they will even kill the mother of the future King of England…

Exactly what happened in Paris on August 30 1997?
Who really killed Princess Diana?
And what is

THE WINDSOR SECRET

ISBN: 978-0-9559911-2-7

Available from *amazon, Lulu* and other online booksellers and thru all good bookshops.

www.ingramcontent.com/pod-product-compliance
Lightning Source LLC
Chambersburg PA
CBHW031102030726

47496CB00002BA/338